FACING OFF

A Novel

Graciela Vaserman Samuels

FACING OFF

A Novel

Graciela Vaserman Samuels

SAMUEL WACHTMAN'S SONS   DEKEL PUBLISHING HOUSE

FACING OFF

Graciela Vaserman Samuels

Copyright © 2016

Dekel Publishing House
www.dekelpublishing.com

North American rights by
Samuel Wachtman's Sons, Inc.
ISBN 978-1-941905-02-9

All rights reserved. No portion of this book, except for brief review, may be reproduced, stored in a retrieval system, or transmitted in any form or by any means – electronic, mechanical, photocopying, recording, or otherwise – without written permission of the publisher. For information regarding international rights please contact Dekel Publishing House, Israel; for North American rights please contact Samuel Wachtman's Sons, Inc., U.S.A.

English translation: Rosemary Wiltshire
Language editing: Kathleen Roman
Cover design: Brice Beauprêtre, Alex Uberti
Cover illustration: Kibbutz by Jose Gurvich (1927-1974)

Cover curatorship, interior design and typesetting by

For information contact:

Dekel Publishing House
P.O. Box 45094, Tel Aviv
6145002, ISRAEL
Tel: +972 3506-3235
Fax: +972 3506-7332
Email: info@dekelpublishing.com

Samuel Wachtman's Sons, Inc.
2460 Garden Road, Suite C
Monterey, CA 93940, U.S.A.
Tel: 831 649-0669
Fax: 831 649-8007
Email: samuelwachtman@gmail.com

To my man, Stanley.

Table of Contents

1. March 2003 9
2. From the Big Apple, Apples, Mimosas, and other Climbers and Climbing Plants 20
3. March 3, 1972 24
4. September 1967 29
5. Going Back 33
6. 1945 44
7. Paris 59
8. Roots and Ruins: Stories to be Told 86
9. July 1974 121
10. The Journey to Córdoba 136
11. Buenos Aires 152
12. Wood Anemones at Tea Time 161

March 2003

The idea of the journey, of these pages, came to me in a complete rush, just as when all of a sudden it becomes clear it can't be any other way. It was simply a matter of changing the position of the kaleidoscope.

A subtle shifting of position, very slightly turning the rainbow pieces in the light, and I could see almost all of it—the tight weave of unstable, complex relations, with ourselves as prisoners forever caught between fantasy, reality, and desire, held down by a demanding present and an empty past, air, and mirage. The questions were so numerous that they caught in my throat until I felt I was suffocating. The thread to at least try to clear a path through the undergrowth and the darkness of the tunnel came to me from old Hillel: "If I don't do it for myself, who will? And if not now, then when?"

I could see there was no other way and so with my three daughters I traveled back to my roots, to Argentina, where I was born.

That's it as far as the physical journey is concerned, because the internal journey had begun long before and with pangs of labor.

While I was planning and fitting all the details together I kept singing, "I've been to paradise but I've never been to me." Don't be for others. Be me and me. The urgings of good old Hillel.

I was perfectly confident I would be able to control my steps and theirs. But I didn't know what I was getting into or what I was looking for. I wanted time and space with my daughters. Three young women with their mother in the same space trying to rediscover one another. I couldn't build a world for them, I know that now, but I could set the scene. I could hold the door ajar and let them enter if they wanted to. The force of curiosity and the novelty of the geography would be the link, the driving force between us. The devil is hidden among the folds, the details and apparitions, but so are the angels.

> *I wake up with a start. The past I am looking for is written in stone. I don't recognize the alphabet. Time and tears are engraving cuneiform characters. I can't decipher them in the desert. Now there are pebbles in the muddy water and I'm thrashing about and shouting. My silence is drowning me.*

We will begin our journey in New York. It will be the point where we all meet up. And from there, we will fly direct to Buenos Aires.

My daughter, Lara, is already in Manhattan. I arrived from Paris.

She is so absentminded, my little redhead. I can see her standing on the corner of 10th and 46th Street where the taxi has dropped me off. She neither sees nor hears me. She's peering intently at the expiration date on the bottle of milk she's holding.

"Lara! It's me, Mommy! Don't you recognize me?" I call, half laughing. She continues peering through her glasses, which are a style typical of the absentminded professor. Her large, green-gray eyes look around…

"Lari, I'm here, in the taxi!"

"Hmm," the kindly African American taxi driver chuckles, "your daughter doesn't see you." He's enjoying the scene. I wonder if he isn't speaking some deeper truth, that my daughter just doesn't see me.

"Hello, Mommy—where did you come from?" As though she really doesn't know from where I came.

So again I say, "Lari, from JFK. Wait a minute, stay there."

I pay the fare, smiling at the driver and making excuses for her—my scientist daughter, she's like that, a little distracted. I feel better as though his complicity is a good omen for starting out on our journey.

"Come here, my Lari, let me give you a hug."

She is small, slight, and fragile. I can hold her in my arms. I kiss her freshly washed hair, which always smells so clean. It's a scent I recognize in myself; it makes me feel at home.

"Mommy, I checked the date on the milk; it's fresh."

"Let's go upstairs and I'll make you some tea."

We walk only a few yards along the sidewalk. The black gate at the entrance gives us an enticing glimpse of the garden around the building. Three steps lead up to two small balconies, set with wrought iron tables and chairs, and wooden benches down one side of the garden. This is where the neighbors give vent to their agreements and disagreements, terrestrial and celestial food; coffee, a letter, a newspaper, a dog, happy or sad news—it all provides a bridge for this very special community.

"Mommy, doesn't this remind you a little of a moshav in Israel with everyone living in their own houses but with a central meeting place, here in the garden? The feeling of loneliness that they say is part of living in big cities like New York, well, we don't have that here, do we?"

* * *

Another flash of the kaleidoscope from the beginning. The image of the prism is bright but at the same time calming.

My youngest daughter, Ayala, lives in northern Israel in a kibbutz surrounded by land just a few kilometers from Lebanon. Many people say that those living on either side of the border greet one another through the natural landscape around them, and that the harmony of nature brings them together. The hills and valleys embrace and tell of secrets shared with no one.

The windows in the kibbutz's communal dining room look north toward Lebanon, west to the Mediterranean, south to Lake Tiberias and Jerusalem, and east toward Jordan. Like everything in the Middle East, taking part depends on where one is sitting.

The greenest olive oil comes from Syrian olive trees, which also grow here. The oil from those olives has the most delicious taste and the olives themselves are succulent. When people are talking about olive oil and someone says, "Ah, Syrian olive oil," that person shows he or she is a real connoisseur. It has always been like that, me finding a way as best I can, among their faces and gestures. In a sea not always as smooth as olive oil, learning how to ride out the storms, the rebellions, and the riots.

* * *

I come back to Lari.

"You're right. Here, behind a healthy respect for others and their space, there is something intangible that goes beyond mere courtesy. It's something to do with a certain feeling of safety and trust."

Lara opens a second large door and very gentle music seems to welcome us.

Heads look up, eyes inspect us, and smiles greet us.

"Good morning. Who have you come to visit?"

We answer. Nodding heads seem to give approval.

It's like that in Ayala's kibbutz. Every new face that appears in the dining room elicits murmured comments. They all know one another but check all the same even though they have an abundance of details about every single person.

There is a profusion of lavender and bougainvillea, which in Buenos Aires we used to call Santa Rita. Very old trees and many olive trees. It is a bio garden, with sculptures everywhere. They believe in open-air museums. Children have fun touching the different shapes and materials of the sculptures.

* * *

As I watch them I can't help thinking of my friend, Fenton, an English diplomat I met at an exhibition in Jerusalem.

I had been admiring a sculpture when he came up to me.

In Jerusalem, every year members of the diplomatic corps with any artistic ability used to show their work in the theater.

Sherover. That is the official name, in honor of its donors, Guita and Milton.

Sherover. For us Jerusalem residents, it will always be the Jerusalem theater.

It was beautiful. I wondered if it was us he had been thinking of.

"Do you like it?" he asked.

"Yes, very much. What a pity I can't touch it. This sculpture is just asking to be touched."

"Touch it then. That's exactly what it wants."

I looked at him in surprise. "But that's not allowed!"

"I'm a diplomat, yes, but my great love is art," he explained. "I began to paint during the years I spent in Moscow. Then my sister lost her sight. I sculpt so she can appreciate what I do. Being able to feel the marble, the wood, the different materials I work with, lets her take part in my life and enjoy with me the beauty that I hope in part it can convey to her."

We went to visit him in his workshop and listened to his stories. We tasted his wife's excellent cooking. Fenton would have praised the objective of Ayala's community to pull down the barriers between art and everyday life.

* * *

The houses on the kibbutz are single story. The people make the furniture themselves. I love to visit the goats they keep and the chicken coop. I was so excited the first time I saw a kid being born.

The horses are farther away.

They make toys for export. They produce goats' milk and the most delicious cheese I have ever tasted.

They raise dogs that help in the therapy of autistic children and other children with social or communication problems.

My daughter works with the dogs. Through the dogs' affection she has managed to reach a level of emotional dialog that has eased her relations with the family. This work has also given her a sense of responsibility and, even more importantly, it has helped her feel and know what is needed.

The Druze festival is a cultural event for people from all over the country. The music and the instruments preserve ancient traditions and the intoxicating rhythm envelops us. These fascinating neighbors of the kibbutz bedeck their villages. What other people can boast of having legendary mystery and hospitality as their main cultural assets? The Arab and Jewish villages in this region mingle in the wind. I like to wander through the narrow, twisting, stone-lined streets, among the men and the women with their white headscarves, where my footsteps seem to echo in silence. Through the great doors carved with Islamic motifs I can see courtyard gardens and smell the scent of coriander and lemon trees.

I taste my first Turkish coffee with cardamom and somehow through the cup I'm holding, I remember some lines by Salman Masalha, the Druze poet who writes in Arabic and Hebrew:

> Day has already flown from memory.
> I remember
> The door that opened onto oblivion.
> It is the door that opens onto
> Rooms of happiness.
> So much remembering makes you forget who you are.
> And between sip and sip
> You will find, in the cloudy bottom of the cup
> That oblivion is the beginning of memory.

* * *

The ground-floor apartment of the building where Lari was staying had no curtains. It made me feel invited to look inside. Colors and furniture greeted me; perhaps they recognized me. In turn, I smiled at them.

Well, if everything could be seen from the outside it must mean they didn't mind people looking in.

Would this be the starting point, the novelist's secret?

"They want to share their life with us, don't they," I said to Lari pointing at the window. But she already knew my interest in this couple.

They were middle-aged. She was a writer and a very good cook. She looked fragile, slim, with very white skin and her hair was tied at the nape of her neck. Deep blue eyes and a small nose from which her transparent glasses seemed to dangle. She was always dressed in a skirt. No one had ever seen her wearing pants. There were cushions with a small blue flower pattern that made me think they must be Bostonians, probably from Massachusetts. There was something that reminded me of the island of Nantucket. I could almost say I could imagine them four hundred years ago arriving on American shores with the *Mayflower*. Yes, she must be a Daughter of the American Revolution, as they called themselves. Strong, direct, hardworking, and guileless.

He was a photographer and art critic for a major New York newspaper. All his photographs were in black and white. He was strong, so much so that I felt his strength through the window—at least that was how it seemed to me. An old television took pride of place in the living room. An enormous 1940s-style lamp lit up the bookcase giving the scene a theatrical quality. One could see a large double bed. The colorful pillows were made of soft material. A bed that seemed to say, "So much has happened and happens here, I hold too many memories and secrets. I am welcoming and give rest to those who seek it and pleasure to lovers who are grateful for my silence."

There were books everywhere, paintings and photographs of the heroes of their lives and of the theater world, in frames of different sizes and colors. Some were signed; many were yellowing with age, grouped around these walls like friends who had gathered together to applaud this couple's life. They were as alive as the heat of the kitchen and the smell of cooking from the oven. The kitchen had racks full of spices. There were flowers on the round dining table. The husband was sitting in the wing chair with its threadbare upholstery, which was the same as that of the velvet cushions. On the wife's dressing table were colored perfume bottles that made little rainbows with the light falling through the window. An old film projector and beautiful rugs told stories of faraway places.

I could imagine flying on them like in the children's stories of the magic carpet and Aladdin's cave with his wonderful lamp or Genghis Khan, or perhaps to the mountains of Afghanistan, that fantastic country stained with so much death.

Always dressed in well-worn jeans and snow-white T-shirt, he walked around barefoot. His blueish-white mane of hair made us think of a lion with his steady, very sensual expression. He had the air of a man who enjoyed beauty and appreciated the aesthetic. He was suntanned; his lined face told of a life full of experiences. His eyes, behind glasses, were steel-gray and cold like those I imagined a hunter's to be. His fingers were long and slender. He was tall. Standing next to his wife he didn't overshadow her but it was more like the image of a large animal protecting its mate.

She was bending over what she was cooking and he was waiting. There was a feeling of harmony and evident attraction.

I stopped looking and stood back. The moment was so intimate I felt I should draw the curtains that weren't there, but in my mind I tactfully gave them curtains.

I felt good. Knowing that the couple would continue with their lives like that gave me confidence in the future.

"Mommy, what's that smile about?" asked Lari.

"Nothing. It's something I don't talk to you about but sometimes I indulge in telling myself stories. It's difficult to explain but I'm happy that 'two characters' of my future story are giving me a helping hand in its construction," I said. "Let's go inside, Lari, I want that cup of tea," I whispered. How could I explain to her, how could I make her enter into my secret antechamber and convey to her all that these people conjured up? They were so well modeled, like Rodin's *Kiss*.

* * *

"Is there something special that seems like Boston to you?" My inquiring, perceptive daughter asks.

"Fairytales, stories from before and some you already know," I explain. A novel you must have studied in literature class, by Henry James. Twenty-five odd years ago they made a film, *The Bostonians*, that met with great success. Well, anyway, I loved it. Already in the days of Henry James on one level you had the shock of cultures with the liberal Bostonian up against the traditions of the South. And overlying that, an inevitably biting criticism of new money. The actress, Vanessa Redgrave, charmed men and women alike.

*　*　*

Ayala was to spend four years in Boston, at Lesley University. It has a program for young people with special needs. Lesley is in Cambridge and the city, small as it is, is almost a replica of the city of the same name in the United Kingdom.

When we went to visit the college for the first time we were struck by the colors—that strong, dark green as though painted on the leaves of the trees and the velvety grass, the red roofs and the white, wooden houses.

Puritan, like those who arrived by boat in 1656, and warm, like the men and women who had the courage to build their freethinking world.

The street names are of those they left behind in their land on the other side of the Atlantic. Their accent retains some British intonations and they still practice direct democracy.

It isn't for nothing that when there are presidential elections in the United States what happens in New Hampshire influences who will become the candidates.

Ayala immediately felt at home in Cambridge. It reminded her of her years spent at school in England. There, where they even respect tea time.

Those were four wonderful years, not only for her but for the whole family. We used to enjoy visiting her and when the time came to say goodbye we felt we were leaving something very close to our hearts.

* * *

I will have to be more specific with what I want to say in spinning this story so that my Lari, who is so organized, doesn't lose patience with my ramblings. One of these days I will show her the Royal Spanish Academy's definition of the word *vaiven*:

From coming and going

1. m. Backwards and forwards movement of a person who after going over a route goes back over the same ground describing it, moving in the opposite direction.
2. m. Unstable variety or inconsistency of things in their duration or achievement.
3. m. Encounter or risk that exposes to ruin what is being attempted, or to failure of what is sought.
4. m. Maritime. Thin rope, painted white or tarred and of two or three strands, that is used to hold and sheath other thicker ones, to be intertwined and make certain textiles.

From the Big Apple, Apples, Mimosas, and other Climbers and Climbing Plants

There's no forgetting the air and the color of a city's sky when it wakes and begins to stretch itself. Dawn. It is almost six in the morning. The streets are being cleaned, the blinds on the café windows are being raised and the chairs arranged around tables soon to be occupied by early risers, who are waiting for the telltale smell of still-warm croissants, fresh from the oven, which gives the signal that baked goods have been placed on the counter at the café on the corner. We must not waste these moments when the city and the day are still pristine.

I'm strolling through Storyland, the land of dreams and ideals, and turning away from the land of worries; it is almost out of reach now along with so many other places. It is like trampling on mirages in which those of the present, always urgent, jumble generalities with specificities, capital letters with lowercase ones. History, with my story. That is one of the hypotheses of this weave. Straight, short stitches, sometimes slightly raised and sometimes a chain stitch. Choose strong colors.

"Are you tired, Mommy?" asks Lara with her innocent expression that makes our hearts melt. Looking at her, I can hardly believe she's already been married for four years.

"No, not very. I slept on the plane, but I'd like to take a shower and brush my teeth." The place hasn't changed since my last visit. The warm atmosphere does me good. Although I don't say so, the stress of the journey suddenly makes me feel tired.

* * *

My decision to travel alone with my daughters was not at first well received by Howard. He felt excluded. I needed to have them with me without his very British view of psychological analysis being only for weak people.

Although my father raised me to believe the saying "Don't be afraid of life," and my mother used to say, "You need to remember where you come from," I never denied emotion.

* * *

"Mommy, why didn't you wake me up?"

My guru, Professor Liz Leyton, always lets her friends stay in her apartment when she's away. She travels a good deal and her nest is an oasis of green, of classical music and windows that open onto the world of books and intellectual rebels from New York's West Side. It was a piano factory built in 1880 and now has been converted into very attractive apartments. We were to enjoy it until our flight to Buenos Aires.

Liz is in Kabul. It's her fifth mission. She works with the Department of Education, trying to establish a curriculum for women and girls. No easy task, but Liz needs such challenges. She is a woman who will not pass through this world without leaving her mark of commitment and fighting for those in need. She is by no means the only one. Many people want to be a part of building a new Afghanistan that seeks its freedom.

The residents of the West Side of New York do not like to be confused with those of the East Side. They have opted to maintain a stunning architectural style in keeping with the colors of the various groups of immigrants and the smells of their cuisines. Everything is spiced with quantities of old bookshops. A violin can be heard playing Mendelssohn. It must be a white-haired Jew of Russian origin, who retains his accent although he arrived here before or just after World War II. It's no surprise to hear an Italian American or African American taxi driver using words like *chutzpah* or *mensch* and many other words that Yiddish has added to everyday New York vocabulary.

That is where there is the best place to find the most exotic cooking ingredients, breads, and coffees. Zabar's. As soon as you set foot in that store you're enveloped in thousands of intoxicating smells that make you want to taste everything. The hot bagels arrive and vanish in an instant and the quality of their pastrami is renowned. On Sunday mornings there is always a line of people waiting outside Zabar's with the inevitable *New York Times* tucked under their arms.

Through New Yorker friends, with whom I would spend summers together with my younger daughter, I learned that, in fact, it is better to buy the *New York Times* on Saturday evenings after the theater and devour it with one's first cup of coffee on Sunday morning. It's a tradition Howard keeps up, thousands of miles away, in London. For him, it is the *Observer* first thing on Sunday morning. I hold on to these private, privileged memories.

"Mommy, why didn't you wake me up?"

"What for? We don't have to rush off somewhere, do we?"

We arrive at the airport very early the next day. It's a habit of mine to arrive early whenever I need to be somewhere, especially when I'm traveling or meeting one of my daughters from their travels. I prefer stations because it's easier to see one another even at a distance. In airports there are such crowds and in bus stations the gas fumes are overpowering. My daughters laugh at me but they do the same thing—arrive early.

It's the sort of thing that mothers pass on to their children.

I have memories of my parents who would surprise us by arriving unannounced.

March 3, 1972

It was a Friday evening and we were getting ready to go downstairs to the dining room.

Shabbat. The communal dining room where we were living before finding our future home was already full of people. The office sent for me and there were my parents.

We were living in Israel.

I was expecting my first baby, Lara, and I should have already given birth. She was overdue. I didn't even know that my parents had been in Europe for their annual business trip. All they said was, "Come and eat with us."

They gave me the name of the hotel where they were staying. Howard was openmouthed. It was his first experience of the surprise effect of which my parents were such experts.

We went to eat with them and the next day traveled to Jerusalem. My parents wanted to say a special prayer at the Western Wall for the birth of my baby. My mother was not religious but she believed in G-d. My father was traditional and very much a believer. Although my mother was the daughter of a rabbi and a Cohen, she was more distant with the subject of religion. My father, who kept up with some traditions, was raised in a Zionist family. His ancestors had already traveled to Palestine by the early nineteenth century and his father, my grandfather, was very active in the European Zionist movement.

The next day, a Sunday, I was admitted to the hospital. Lara was born twelve hours later. Everyone looked pale and tired but I felt wide awake and full of energy.

"Gabriela, don't you think the baby's fingernails are wonderful?" asked my mother.

"Yes...."

"Doesn't it seem like a perfect manicure?"

"Yes, she's my daughter."

"No, Gabriela, it's a miracle. Every baby who's born is a miracle of the Almighty."

I didn't know what to say.

Many years later I understood. That was the only birth that I had my parents with me.

I ask myself whether in some far-off, hidden moment, I will be abandoned and perhaps that is why I always insist on arriving earlier than I need to. Perhaps on this journey I will also find an answer to my anxiety about time and urgency.

* * *

Lara is looking at the list of arrivals, which says the plane is expected to land as scheduled. There is time for coffee.

Around us we can hear people speaking Hebrew.

> *I always have a special feeling when an El Al plane arrives. Even today, the Israeli airline is still a sort of miracle for us. We never stop admiring it and each person who arrives is somehow "our" passenger. I don't know how to explain it but I can assure you that we all look at one another in that special moment when people are reunited with their family or friends as though they*

were our own; we know them and welcome them. I don't deny it, sometimes tears of happiness or emotion come to our eyes.

Happiness. That's all. Do we feel like that because our people have arrived? That we continue to exist? That there is a future? David Grossman said that Israeli writers have "a sense of urgency." Perhaps it is a need to record the moment, words engraved in case we disappear. Is that what they feel, what we feel? Some imperative needs to register and inscribe the moment before it disintegrates with time and the destruction of our existence, so ephemeral and controlled by seemingly never-ending wars. When one is over, another begins. So we need to leave testimonies, testimonies of those fleeting moments and events that have actually taken place and are not a mere figment of our imaginations, to ensure they are transmitted to our descendants as our ancestors did, those of the Bible, Masada, and so many other documents. Is that why we love books and they call us the People of the Book? I don't know.

We are constantly seeking ourselves, trying to recognize ourselves, whether through words or stones, striving to identify in the desert or the hills, in the sea and in the silence that speaks to us of other legends and of our people.

"The plane has landed, Lari, people are already coming through. Look, those are Israeli duty free bags…look, look, where are they?"

I know my voice is anxious and my face must be showing it too. I try to master my emotion. Lara puts her small, soft hand in mine. Among the jeans, the luggage, and the fashionably dressed are the religious men with their big hats and long black coats. The feeling is the same with everyone and it is as though we are all at the same family gathering. Before, there were more words for saying basically the same thing—stateless, landless, expatriate, refugee, missing, colonized, shunned—because almost always, in the beginning migration is the product of need, ill-treatment, and violence that creeps imperceptibly over borders. There is no solution to the needs that lie so much deeper than merely the surface. Those needs arise with the first unspoken insult. Disappearances are caught and avenged in dreams we hurriedly blot out with talk. With rage and isolation by the shovelful.

In order to try to explain this feeling, we only need reread to those close to us part of a letter from Freud written in 1938 during the *Anschluss*, the annexation of Austria by the German Reich:

Perhaps, with regard to what a migrant feels in such a painful way, to you. He needs to understand one thing. It is a question of losing the language he has always breathed and thought and which he will not be able to replace with any other, despite all his efforts to adopt a new one. For me, it is painful to realize that in English, although I well know how to express myself, I feel thwarted and like it (the id) tries to resist yielding to the Gothic script I'm used to.

Some old photographs of key moments of our history come to mind. The arrival of refugees in Palestine, coming off the boats with skull-like faces and ragged clothing, their eyes shining, searching for some familiar face—a relative or fellow inmate from the camps—who might have survived the Shoah, and perhaps that face is there among those other hundreds of eyes searching the sea of faces and memories for someone with the identity of a name and a past.

The Jews of Yemen thought that the plane taking them to Israel was a magic carpet. Their whole existence had been centered around reading the prayers of Sidur and hearing the legends passed from one generation to the next of the greatness and power of the Lord. Their journey to Israel, flying on a plane through clouds, seemed a miracle.

Refugees from Ethiopia left behind hundreds of dead as they journeyed along a desert road. They followed the route taken by their queen of Sheba when she returned from Jerusalem bringing with her the beliefs of the Jewish people. Now their heirs have come home.

And then there are those who, like me, arrive with no baggage, happy and fearless. Through conviction, we return to our land to be ourselves, each person with his or her cultural background learned over centuries of exile, to resume where our ancestors had left off.

But we are all united in the one drive to create, to build, to meet together through our histories in a new life; at least that is our aim.

September 1967

I remember the photos of when I arrived in Buenos Aires as a newlywed. My parents' expressions, the happiness on my mother's face, the curiosity in the eyes of my brother, Ariel, and the hidden emotion of my father.

I try to reconstruct the three months I spent with them after the wedding. An experience I recommend to no one. It was the most unfair situation I could have inflicted on Howard. For the first time he had to face a world very different from his own. Despite having read books and been interested in politics and history, and having listened to anecdotes of my childhood and all my grumbling, nothing could have been further from reality.

My family was dry, distant, and critical. My parents were happy—at least, so they said. They had met Howard in Jerusalem and his parents in London. But that was not enough for him to become an additional member of the family. The test was yet to come.

It was always going to happen, do what one might to satisfy that measure of the perfect ideal that was, therefore, out of reach.

* * *

Waiting for someone in a station, an airport, the street, or just sitting in a café, everything is tinted with our feelings for the person for whom we're waiting: desire, hope, the unknown, union or separation.

"Mommy, there they are! Look, can you see them?"

Lara always manages to bring me back to reality, more or less intact.

Two tired faces, Noemia, my second daughter, and Ayala, my youngest. I see their eyes searching for us and then their faces light up.

Laughter and talking all at the same time. It seems none of us is listening but it doesn't matter. We understand one another so well.

Without saying anything, Ayala looks for the "goody bag" she had asked for in an email, saying "it would be nice if" I could buy them apples, plums, M&Ms, gum, potato chips, and a whole list of other treats for the journey.

"Don't worry, it's all in my bag," I say and Ayala smiles at me. Once again, I haven't failed her.

They look at me, waiting for me to tell them how they are going to take part in the continuation of the adventure. I watch their small faces, three little soldiers, three babies in my arms. The images become confused.

We check our baggage for the flight to Argentina, which always leaves well after nightfall.

Once everything was sorted out and with no further introduction, I decided to give them an outline of what I had already mentally prepared. The world around us melted away.

I leave aside my "presentation." I can't hide it, they know I want to tell them and they don't say anything.

Ayala, the youngest, looks at Noemia, the one with the romantic eyes. Her expression seems to say, "Oy, oy, oy, wait for it, let's see what we're in for."

"First of all I want to set a few parameters," I say, looking at them. They don't look surprised. Their understanding of one another is tangible. I know I'm smiling. Their laughter doesn't surprise me.

"All right, now we don't have to be serious about it, but please, just listen to me for a few minutes, will you?"

They begin to eat without saying anything. The laughter and chatter from the other tables clearly doesn't bother them. Most of the other people in the restaurant are Latin Americans who will probably be on the same flight as us.

I could hear my own voice. It sounded strange, almost nervous. It was as though I was about to make a speech.

"We already know, Má, order and…" Lara says. Being the oldest she takes the initiative and the other two defer to her.

Around us, travelers are eating hamburgers, hot dogs, and chips as though it were their last meal. The smells float among the seemingly different languages but which, in fact, are all the same language with varying accents. Central America mixed with South America.

It was impressive. Suddenly my body understands everything. There is no need to translate. The terminal is full of color, atmosphere, and happiness. Exuberance is in the air, wrapping around everyone in a little waltz of the past.

The one I remember and hum to myself is from the beginning of the last century, "Desde el alma." The Uruguayan Rosita de

FACING OFF – Graciela Vaserman Samuels

Meló was only fourteen when she wrote it. The words still help me:

> Soul, if they have hurt you so much
> Why don't you let yourself forget?
> Why do you prefer
> Crying about what you have lost,
> Searching for what you have loved,
> And calling out to what has died?

Going Back

We separate without a tear…

Tango by Cadícamo and Tinelli

* * *

I would like them to see me as a woman and forget that I'm their mother. I want honesty and the right to change plans if we can all agree to it.

But how can I ask them not to see me as their mother? What am I looking for? I know. Perhaps I should just go ahead and spell it out.

While they are talking among themselves, ignoring my presence, I'm wondering if that is what it would be like.

"Please, I need you to…"

"What are you trying to say, Ma?" Noemia asks, surprised.

"What I want to say is that I need you to judge me. Not like in a trial but I want, that is, I don't want you to simply accept everything I tell you. I want you to ask me questions, as many questions as you like."

"Mommy, do you want us to talk about everything?" asks Ayala.

"Yes, that as well. I don't want there to be any secrets or holding back."

"Mommy, do you want us to help you find the Gabriela who left this country thirty-five years ago? Is that it?"

"Yes, Lara, that's what I want."

"I like the idea. What do you think, Ayala? We're going to see what Mommy was like when she was young and we'll talk about everything, inside and out. Are you all right with that?"

"Yes, and I'll keep a diary; it can be our travel log," Ayala said.

The rest seems out of my control. I'm watching a film and wondering how it will end. Sometimes it's in color, sometimes just black and white.

They dim the lights to let passengers sleep if they want to. I can't and I don't even think I want to.

I get up to look at my daughters. Lara is asleep, curled up like a little cat. Noemia sees me looking at them. It's so true, what Carla my friend from Helsinki once said to me when she saw Noemia years and years ago: "Gabriela, that daughter of yours was born with the wisdom of old age."

She doesn't need to say anything. Noemia just looks at me and her silent words say, "Keep calm, Mommy, we're with you, we'll be patient, we want to listen to you and hear what you have to say. We're not going to fight over silly things."

I smile at her, trying to reach for her soft, smooth hand.

I feel better. Beside me, Ayala is snoring gently. With the time difference and the emotion of it all, this young woman, whose character is so strong and very stubborn, feels at ease. Small beads of perspiration on her forehead. Beautiful. I adore her.

I wonder if there will be problems at passport control. I'm traveling with my British passport, which says, "Place of birth: Argentina." Will they let me into the country? Why am I so frightened? Clearly, for me, although I've been back to Argentina so many times during the thirty-five years since I left that country, I still feel mistrust about everything and my fears are many and dark. I must sleep.

What will happen when my elder sister, Dora, sees them? We are not close in the slightest. She asks me to be her friend. How can I be when I don't feel affection for her nor can I talk to her normally? Well, anyway, my rabbi will be there, and Dora and I won't see that much of each other. We'll just spend Friday night there and Saturday we'll set off for the south. Shortening the visit will avoid problems. Although in this Gordian knot, my problems are the same old ones. So why am I coming back now?

If it weren't for the sound of the engines and the smell of the plane that permeates everything and lasts for weeks, this could well be a recurring dream with tinges of nightmare. A maze where it's impossible to find the way out. A pathway lost among official buildings, paint peeling off the walls. Empty. How can I know if the guide who has just appeared is an angel or an evil imposter? Stifling heat wakes me up in time and as though it were manna I'm grateful for the noxious liquid handed out by the indifferent, professional air hostess.

Every now and then I check my atlases, going over the maps with a magnifying glass. I follow the lines of rivers with my fingers; sometimes I can't even see them but rather I avoid them, that is, when I would prefer to be like a *yuyo* that flowers in rock crevices. No one knows how it can grow at all, like feathers in the wind. Others would trace my tracks, our past, with a red marker, indelible like veins. It's time to fold up the maps of the Encyclopædia Britannica, to search in the valley of the Dniester River, the source of the beginning and the end of all life's sweetness and pain.

On either side, on both banks of the river, are cities like needles in very small font with just a few in all capital letters: Braila, Sibiu,

Chisinau, Odessa, Kracow, Lodz. In Argentina, Jewish families are close but separated not by rivers but by rifts of poverty. Those who succeeded in life have gravestones in the Liniers cemetery, while those who did less well are buried in the Ciudadela cemetery. And now vandals have desecrated both cemeteries and broken the flowerless vases. They urinate on the gravestones and the weeds have eaten away at the names inscribed in black ink. More than fifty years ago, my sobs were carried off in the wind. But as I am the granddaughter, I'm sure they will forgive me for visiting them so seldom. But no one can see me because I'm crying alone, in the back, suddenly for you and for me.

Most of the tombstones in the Liniers cemetery are marble and those in the Ciudadela cemetery are black granite, but there are also many that are blocks of cement.

Later, when the Reaper needed more space, they put us in the cheaper Tablada cemetery, the equivalent of a discount store. Those buried in the Liniers cemetery were better off than those in the Ciudadela cemetery or they had been there for longer. Among ourselves, people who commit suicide cannot be laid to rest with everyone else and they are buried separately, in the worst space available, usually somewhere difficult to get to, against a weak wall as though they weren't already vulnerable when they were alive. They do not accept the principle of G-d gives and G-d takes away (life).

Can we honestly say that at any time in the pretentiously bourgeois neighborhoods of Reina del Plata we were ever at ease?

> I must admit that I never felt the subject of this book was of any particular interest, but now I find myself simply curious to see if I'll have the necessary courage to get to the end.
>
> Groucho Marx, from **Groucho and Me**

The dream had disappeared. Twelve hours of traveling had gone by. We were all wide awake and expectant. I looked at the faces of my little women. How will they take to all this? Is it so very different from the world they live in? Am I afraid they'll judge where I was born and grew up? Am I or am I not a reflection of this society? Am I the mother in Paris or Jerusalem or am I the other person, the one who left here more than thirty years ago? Will I be loyal to them as well as to my past? If it isn't a matter of answering all these questions, which are so hard for me, then what am I— what are we—doing here? Stepping out of the plane I felt the heat on my head but not on my body.

It strikes me as strange that with all the changes that have happened, place names have remained the same.

I show them the new towns built during the time of Perón, small, identical houses with red roofs, a town square and a church. Now they are smeared with age and poverty. They are not interested. But they see horses trotting in the fields and that impresses them.

"Noemia, go and get a cart for the luggage and Lari, come with me and we'll divide up the money I exchanged. Noemia, watch where those suitcases are going...."

I tell myself, *Be careful, Gabriela. Put your ear to the ground and listen for the rhythm they're asking for. Recognize the language and try not to lose your way. The trotting horse will show you the way home.*

That's how my father's assistant Don Segura used to talk to me when we were in the countryside.

Don Segura, I've traveled a good deal, I've seen many things, I've been through good times and bad.

Will I recognize my horse's gait and will I trust him? And what about him? Will he recognize me?

"Señora, shall we go straight to the hotel?" the driver asks.

"No, to the Liniers cemetery. I want to visit my family."

I wanted to start this journey at the beginning, with my—and their—ancestors.

"Mommy," I feel her hand rather than hear her voice. It's Ayala, giving me support and love.

I realize I had been walking so quickly I'd left them behind.

The cemetery is very quiet. The trees hardly move in the almost imperceptible breeze.

"Sorry, girls," I say, slowing down.

They follow me in silence—not a sad silence, just respectful.

Each of my daughters has separately taken part in the annual March of the Living, in Poland. They have visited the concentration camps, so it is not a cemetery with family tombs that is going to move them.

I can't find the way. I have to ask, so I knock on the cemetery keeper's door.

"Excuse me, could you please tell me how to get to the Goldemberg family plot?"

He looks at me, takes off his cap, and asks, "Who are you, Señora?"

I answer, barely audible, "I'm Gabriela Goldemberg."

"Ah, you're the one who lives abroad then? Come with me."

There they are in front of me. My parents and my brother, Ariel. The family plot and I couldn't see it. I can feel my daughters almost wrapped in my arms. I don't know if I should pray—what would I say?—or cry? No tears fall from my eyes.

I hug them fiercely. And I begin to talk and tell them about those who are buried here, and about me, and we visit other graves—my grandparents, uncles, and aunts—and I explain that for over a century our family was here in this country.

I don't cry but kept talking. My *bobe*'s eyes are looking inside me. Bright eyes in the photo on the headstone; just as I remember them. That little woman, her hair neatly in a bun, with an incredibly wide forehead, always dressed in black, full skirts and polished black shoes. She was stern, demanding, and seemed to keep her distance from everyone. I can't remember having given her more than a kiss on the cheek. My father used to kiss her hand.

And yet, yes, I did hear her laugh. Her laughter tinkled like bells. My mother's laughter was the same. When my Ayala laughs it reminds me of that other laughter that died many years ago.

I can remember the smell of *bobe*'s kitchen when she was preparing *knishes*, which my father loved. He would eat them piping hot, straight from the oven. He would laugh and his eyes would water. He always burned his tongue. You could see the face of the spoiled child he had been and that he had known how to keep his self-assured look, never bitter despite all the suffering he endured and never forgot.

Mamá.

On the patio of her apartment, under the steps that led onto the terrace, there stood a barrel of salted cucumbers. I used to love them. She was the only grandmother I knew. I didn't know my grandfathers.

My grandfather was beside her. He looked stern but his eyes were dark, gentle, and understanding. All the relatives were nearby, having sown the soil of America[1] with their tragicomedies.

---

1 All uses of the word "America" refer to South America, unless otherwise indicated.

As tradition dictates, we wash our hands before leaving the cemetery.

The keeper comes up to me, looks at me, and says, "You're a Goldemberg. I knew your father and your mother. They were good people. Señora, I was so sorry for the death of your brother. He was an angel, always smiling."

"Thank you, thank you very much."

"Mommy, did you know everyone we visited?" asks Noemia.

"No, only some of them. Society, family life was very different then. Children and young people were not as close to their elders. And in fact I come from a rather formal family. Haven't you noticed?" It is the best explanation I can give them.

They laugh.

"Were you really naughty and did they punish you?" Ayala asks. "Like Deborah in my school at Milton House when she talked back and they sent her to the dormitory without supper."

I enjoy hearing them chatter away. Their enthusiasm is so soothing.

"Let's leave the dead to rest in peace. They deserve it."

We arrive at the hotel hungry and thirsty. Our rooms are across from each other. We have fun running across the hall from one to the other. Like soldiers, they prepare their suitcases for the journey south, leaving other belongings for the north.

Barbara, from the travel agency, comes to see us. We now have our tickets. She is the person who made all the travel arrangements for us. We are meeting in person for the first time. She was recommended to me by Howard's office in Buenos Aires.

She is very patient with us and answers all our questions. I think she was a little surprised when she met the four of us. Not quite the kind of group she'd been expecting. I think she was rather intrigued by us.

Noemia's and Lara's Spanish is bizarre to say the least. We all laugh. Ayala is watching and listening to them and absorbing some of the language; she also gives it a try.

The hotel is in the Barrio Norte, not very far from my parents' old house, my sister's house, and the synagogue where we were to meet up before the evening meal.

We leave the hotel, walking along the Avenida Santa Fe. When I was young it was considered to be the most elegant of Avenidas. It has changed a good deal since my last visit to Buenos Aires when I came to see my brother.

It had already lost some of its style by then. The shop owners spoke of the serious economic situation and the number of advertisements of apartments for sale, implying the owners were moving out to cheaper areas of the city. An overall air of dusty grayness seems to suggest the difficulties have not yet been overcome. That kind of despondency seems endemic in my city. Did I say *my* city?

We go into a café across from the Plaza San Martín, filled with smoke and the smell of barbecued meat and fried potatoes. We eat hungrily. People look at us because they hear us speaking in English. At that time Argentina wasn't a popular tourist venue; it had yet to become safer from the political point of view.

We can already hear them reciting the prayers for Shabbat when we arrive at the synagogue. The rabbi looks up with a quick smile. I look for my sister among the faces of the congregation. She hasn't arrived yet. The rabbi's wife gestures to us to come and sit beside her. I feel Lara's hand on my arm. I smile at my children and each take a prayer book from a stack in an old cupboard.

We are in the small synagogue. The big one, which has an organ, is closed. Not so many people come nowadays. I can see my father's white head in front of me and I can feel the presence of my mother saying, "Gabriela, your back. Stand up straight!" I straighten up and feel my daughters doing the same. We begin to follow the service. Dora arrives later on. She looks worried. She comes up to us and hugs us. Behind his glasses the rabbi sees it all. I look at him and he seems to say, "Behave yourself. Remember who you are!"

When the service is over, my sister introduces us to people nearby. I get some strange looks. They mistake me for my sister Adela. My daughters don't say a word. The rabbi's wife gestures for us to follow her out.

"Mommy, can we come back to visit the temple inside?"

"Of course we can."

The rabbi comes up to us and invites them to come back and see him. Lara answers in Hebrew.

"Yes, we would like to come. We have so many questions to ask you. When would it be convenient for you?"

"Call me when you get back from your trip. Shabbat shalom."

We get to Dora's house. When she opens the door she shows us the table set for the Shabbat meal. The air is heavy. It all looks so artificial and I can sense the tension around my daughters. To make conversation I try to joke about our journey. Silly jokes that don't break the ice.

Then Ayala gives Dora a small box tied with a ribbon.

"Auntie, it's from all of us, Lara, Noemia, and me. We hope you like it."

Dora looks at them with surprise and unwraps the present. It's a pendant with Hebrew characters spelling *chai*, life, and which correspond to the number eighteen, the luckiest number according to tradition.

"Thank you. I have presents for you too."

They receive their presents and the acting continues until Noemia breaks through the sham by beginning to ask questions about my parents, me, and the whole family. Lara is glowing and Ayala is listening.

I want to run away. It has turned into a nightmare, a series of awful stories in which the hero is my father. She humiliates not only me but my mother as well. When Noemia can't take any more and asks Dora to talk of my grandmother, she says there is no point, that she was irritating and that my grandfather suffered on account of her.

I soon reach my breaking point and with the excuse that we have to be up at dawn the next day, we thank her and leave.

I don't think she understood. She lives in her own world of selective, stifled memories, discarding any that don't fit the puzzle that suits her. I realize I've put my daughters through a rough evening. Not just because she humiliated me both as a sister and as a mother, but because of all that and the vitriolic attack on our mother, I simply wanted to shout at her about the sheer misery it was to be her sister.

I dream that I lose the coat I just bought. All the time, either in dreams or when I'm awake, I have a constant fear of losing some item of clothing and I retrace my steps. What Garden of Eden am I looking for? There is an original sin but there is neither a natural nor an artificial paradise. I'm looking for a new coat that will wear well. Elementary, my dear Watson.

1945

She wakes up and sees her mother smiling at her. María, the nanny, is standing in front, by the door, keeping her distance. Her arms are folded over the belt of her blue-striped uniform. She is also smiling.

White with cold and transparent, the sun shines in through the window, lighting up the room.

It is a big room with toys and a dollhouse at the other end from where Gabriela sleeps. Storybooks on the shelves are neatly stacked like everything else in the family's life.

Her mother, Doña Perlita, as the household staff call her, reaches out to her little daughter, the youngest of six children. The fingernails of her plump hands are painted deep red. She is sleekly groomed with not a hair out of place. A reddish comb shines in her hair, which seems to be higher each time, making her seem taller. She is of small build, which is why she wears high heels. She is always impeccably dressed when she goes out.

"What happened, what did I do?" asks the little girl, but she doesn't actually use words because she's only three and can hardly talk yet.

"You've had a baby bottle long enough, my Gabriela. Now you have to learn how to drink your milk like a big girl."

Gabriela looks pleadingly at María—you love me, María, you know all my little secrets. Where's my bottle?

*   *   *

The kaleidoscope keeps turning. We're traveling by boat to Uruguay. I can remember walking along the deck a lot, holding my father's hand. I know I was wearing a pink outfit with a matching little hat and I was holding a doll.

We're going to Uruguay for the summer holidays. I can remember being out on the upper deck because as soon as I went below, inside the boat, the movement made me seasick. It's still the same today.

We're going to a place called Piriápolis. I'm sharing a room with my sister, Juana. In the mornings, the nanny takes us down to breakfast. My parents have gone out riding. We're standing in front of the elevator waiting for them to come back. I wet myself and Juana laughs at me. They change my clothes and I want my bottle.

I still have a photograph of that journey, the first one I can remember. Over the years we often made that journey. They used to say "crossing the *charco.*" The *charco* was the River Plate—two hundred–odd kilometers wide. Uruguay used to be called the Switzerland of the River Plate. But since then, successive dictatorships have erased such a peaceful nickname and on both shores state terrorism wreaked havoc among the youth of the two countries. Still alive, they were hurled into the water, making them dive to their deaths.

*   *   *

Today, while I am walking in Paris, I suddenly feel I am traveling back to the past. The feeling is so strong that for a brief moment I think, *There's my mother.*

"Natán, summer is coming," she says.

My father smiles, looks at her, and already knows what's coming next. Whether times were good or not so good, there were certain customs they respected and kept.

"I was in Harrods the other day and they already have the season's new collection of sundresses. Then I went by California, you know, the shoe shop on the Avenida Santa Fe. They have sandals with little heels in a range of pastel shades—they're very fashionable this year."

My father listens to her. In those days he still smoked a pipe. He puts down his paper, smiles, and says, "Well then, why don't you go along with Adela and choose something?"

My mother smiles like a young girl who's being allowed to do something naughty.

She begins to laugh in the way only she knows how to do. Her laughter is like the sound of bells, tinkling bells.

Only now have I come to realize that in Paris there is that same style of low-cut sundresses with full skirts and shoulder straps that leave the back bare. Women wearing that style of summer dress have an air of country and sunshine about them.

* * *

There came a time when we couldn't travel any more. It was for political reasons. Perón did not have good relations with Uruguay and all those who opposed his regime sought exile there. Later on, my family would return to Uruguay and have a summer home in Punta del Este. I wasn't living in Argentina by then, but I did visit the flat with my daughters when they were very small. It gave me the strangest feeling.

My mother was so proud of her daughter's fair hair. She loved brushing it, plaiting it, and tying the plaits with large bows to match the dress I was wearing. I was always formally dressed and wore a pinafore so I wouldn't get my clothes dirty. I looked at my mother almost defiantly with large, almost black eyes. I was slim and they told me I would grow to be tall.

My father was the youngest of six, my mother the youngest of seven, and I was the youngest of six children. There was an indescribable complicity among us. An understanding of what it feels like to be the youngest child in a large family.

My nanny, María, was Spanish. She came to Argentina from Galicia after the Civil War. She had shiny gray hair, which she pulled back into a bun at the nape of her neck. Her skin was very white and smooth. Some of her teeth were missing. She had pale eyes and neither smiled nor talked very much, but when she did talk, it was about the land she left behind when she sailed to America, the promised land. She said that there was so much suffering in her home town and that many people died. The Spanish Civil War was a dreadful time for the whole country but for the people of Galicia, that far-away, inward-looking region, conditions were particularly bad. Galicians are hardworking, hard like the climate and the wind that blows in from the Atlantic onto the rocky coast. The houses are built of stone, the religion is hard and the land difficult to cultivate. Galicians feel themselves to be a race apart from the rest of Spain. On the whole, even today there are no motorways or means of communication linking Galicia to the rest of Spain. There is so much hunger. It is this hunger that drives Galicians to emigrate, promising themselves they will return one day. They keep the traditions and values of their homeland and never stop feeling that that is where they belong, just as Galicia continues to wait for the return of her people.

María had a married sister, Juanita, the only sister she ever talked about, and that sister had a daughter called Carmen. Carmen was smaller than me and liked playing with me. She had dark hair, very pale skin, and very big, dark eyes that were always shining. I liked it when they came to visit. It made me feel important to have someone smaller than me to give lessons to and explain how to feed dolls. Carmen and her mother lived outside the city. They had to catch a train and then walk from the station to their house, which was still under construction. The road they walked along was just earth under foot; there was no asphalt and hardly any cars. It was where many immigrants lived, especially those from Spain. Even the houses they built resembled those they left behind so far away.

Argentina is a country of immigrants. The Italians built their own community in a very short span of time, as did the Spanish, the Jews, and the Germans. I was unaware of any problems or hostilities there may have been among the different communities. Each community had schools, hospitals, orphanages, clubs, and charitable organizations for helping those they had left behind in their countries of origin. They regularly held crowded dances to celebrate their traditional festivals. Those Argentinians who had been in the country longer gave nicknames to the newcomers and they were not always very positive. Italians were called *Tanos* and all Jews were called *Rusos*. It didn't matter where they had come from; they were all called *Rusos*. Every Spaniard was referred to as *Gallego* even if he or she'd been born in the Canaries or Andalucía. It was that range of cultural backgrounds that gave the city of Buenos Aires in the early 1900s—and even more so during and after World War II—such color, humor, music, food, and humanity. It all came together to contribute to the country's economic and cultural development and basically to the creation of what is known today as the Buenos Aires–born *porteño*.

For years they thought they could survive despite the hunger, the wars, and persecutions, but then gradually the dream of building a better life for themselves on the other side of the Atlantic became reality. The hope of being able to return to Europe someday was always floating around the talk in cafés, in the names of all the restaurants, businesses, and shops they opened in order to improve family situations. It was the best way to learn about the real geography of Europe.

My family arrived in the early 1900s. They escaped from Russia. The 1905 pogroms and the first stirrings of the Revolution of 1917 forced them to leave for South America.

Juanita's husband, Manuel, was building their house himself. Each time they went there he showed them the progress he had made. I discovered a different world. Even what they eat was different. Boiled meat, potatoes, green beans, and carrots were served up all together in broth, in a soup dish. And they also ate something they called *judías*, which I couldn't understand at all. It almost offended me. My family is Jewish (*judía*) so how could Carmen and her family eat what they call *judías* (Jewish girls)? At home we call those beans *chauchas*. Many years later, I learned the beans had that name because when Jews lived in Spain, they ate them.

That stew became the traditional Monday meal for the new arrivals from Spain, especially during the damp winter months. The stew was meat-based (not the most expensive variety) with an assortment of vegetables and, if possible, a Spanish chorizo. It all took hours to cook. Over time, instead of red meat they used chicken, which they thought made the dish more *porteño*. It became fashionable for people who did not eat the stew at home to go to the Abasto Market and eat it there after an evening at the theater on Saturdays. Some people looked down on such food as being very working class but others would eat it with the feeling that they were thus on a level with the lower social classes.

At Juanita's house, the tablecloth was plastic, patterned with red and white checks. The table they ate at every day was in the kitchen. There was another one in a room where no one ever went. In that room the armchairs and the dining chairs all had thick, transparent plastic covers. They only used that room on very special occasions. It was hot in the kitchen, never cold. The rest of the house was dark and very quiet. Once a week the housewife cleaned and dusted, though there was no dust. She looked at each piece of furniture and with great care she admiringly touched every item they had bought but never used. When I needed to go to the bathroom it was so cold in there it frightened me. But in the kitchen all the windows were misted over with condensation. In the oven there was a cake baking, for tea time. What I liked best were the *buñuelos*—deep-fried batter—and when they were lifted out of the pan they had to be coated by turning them over in a shallow bowl of sugar and then you ate them with milky coffee. Sometimes they were so hot they burned your lips and your tongue but few people could resist them—they were so delicious! And then there were also *churros*, which were more difficult to make. You could buy them at bakeries or cafés and eat them with hot chocolate. It was typical winter fare. It is still usual to eat them in Spain. In Argentina it became an elegant custom to serve *churros* and hot chocolate at the end of a party around four or five in the morning before all the guests went home.

All the other houses in the area were the same: single story, square houses with gardens of flowers and vegetables. The people were drawn together according to the regions of Spain they came from—Galicia, Catalunya, or the Basque Country—and had made or rebuilt a new Spain in the new land of America.

The men worked on building sites as bricklayers and a few were carpenters or electricians. Most of the women took in sewing but some of them went out to work in offices or factories. They had the reputation of being good, decent women with whom city people could leave their children because they knew they would take proper care of them. Gradually, these women progressed to food shops, importing dark green olive oil from Andalucía, olives and dried fish, anchovies in brine, and the famous Spanish chorizo. It was much later that they began importing Rioja and Jerez. The second generation of immigrants from Spain had the support and encouragement of their parents to study and take up posts in government bureaucracy, minor government posts, or careers in science. Then after another generation, there came politicians like Aramburu and Landaburu. Others attained posts in the army and became presidential candidates, but they never forgot their backgrounds or the land of their ancestors. The aspirations of those immigrants were, of course, reflected in the culture of the time, in literature and songs. There were some words of tango songs that spoke of the pride of parents who praise the fact that their son had a highly polished brass plaque on the door with the abbreviation "Dr." in front of his name—an aspiration summed up in the title of Florencio Sánchez's "*M'hijo el dotor* [sic]" (My Son the Doctor).

María talked to her sister Juanita in a caring yet very authoritative way and those who didn't know her might think she was annoyed. She didn't use that tone of voice in my house. María was older than her sister and she was a widow. She never spoke of her husband or where or how he died. She never had children. She wanted to keep the family together. She was a woman who had suffered. She was thin and never wore makeup or changed her hairstyle. The clothes and shoes she wore were always of sober, dark colors with starched white collars, like a nun, and yet when she smiled everything about her lit up.

Juanita was quite the opposite with her easy smiles and jokes. There was happiness and hope in her life. She was not as pretty as María but she had friends among her neighbors who came on Sundays to eat her paella and drink her bottles of good wine. She arrived in Argentina before her sister and did not go through the suffering of the Civil War. It seemed as though she needed María's forgiveness for not having endured the hardship or seen so much death. They didn't talk about their parents. There seemed to be a certain sense of shame and perhaps something of fear in remembering those they left behind in their homeland.

Controversial studies have been carried out on first and second generation immigrants with opinions that sometimes struggle to find a balance between the right to become American with the duty and pride of parental heritage. The findings have varied along with national policies and the establishment with regard to a certain number of factors, but one that stands out is exclusion.

It was many years before I visited Galicia, Juanita and María's homeland. I say "homeland" because that is how they felt about it, how all Galicians feel about it. When they gaze out toward the Atlantic, to one side is England and to the other, America. Many of the colors of the English countryside and the stone with which they build their houses are essentially the same despite being in such different worlds. Those who gaze toward America sometimes shed tears for all the loved ones who seldom return, all those who went away to America to work and send money back to their families who had so little and suffered so much.

I met Elena in her own country, Galicia. She told me about the ways of her people, their strength and resilience, learned through constant struggling against the wind and the stony ground. Waves broke against the rocks of Galicia, that much-loved land, so proud of its history. Hundreds of years ago there was a flourishing Jewish community in Galicia. The local population spoke of them with respect and admiration. There, among the hills and rocks and the land farmed by brave men and women, there was a Jewish population that had escaped from those who were persecuting them for merely being Jewish. There they lived, worked, wrote, and were accepted in Galicia.

Elena shared with me the roots of her people without disguising or hiding anything. I listened to her and wanted to know more. Even now, I am still learning about these people who arrived on the shores of the River Plate and dug their spades into the rich black soil of Argentina, making it their own through their labor.

"María, tell me, why is my mother lying down in the dark?"

"Your mother gets headaches. It's what they call the change of life. Don't make any noise and go back to your room. Finish your homework."

"What is the change of life?"

"Why do you ask so many questions, child?"

She turned away and went back to her sewing. María was always busy doing something or other.

"Will you teach me how to sew? Please, please!" I begged her.

She had three front teeth missing and her sister Juana caled her "Rotten Teeth." She tried not to let it show that her teeth were missing but sometimes she forgot.

"That's enough now. You have other things to do." María's face showed just the hint of a smile.

How sweet that little girl is, but how lonely she feels, thought the woman who never had any children of her own. She stroked my hair and gave me a quick kiss. I put my arms round María's neck.

"María, shall we go to the park? I promise I'll be good."

María got ready to go out. She didn't go out of the house in her uniform. She brushed my hair and held my hand, not letting go until we reached the park. I liked the swings best and I looked happy with my dress flying in the wind, higher and higher.

"María, what's that black carriage with the four black horses and the flowers?"

"That's the princesses' carriage," María answered without looking at me.

"Princesses? Are there really princesses here?"

Silence. I didn't ask her again; I didn't want to annoy María. But María's answer made me dream. Did she mean princesses like in the fairytales? Then did that mean Snow White and Cinderella really were true stories?

Today I'm asking you, María, you who went through so much sadness and hunger, how were you able to say such a beautiful thing and have such a generosity of spirit? Much later, life taught me that those weren't princesses' carriages but hearses.

When I arrived in Buenos Aires for the first time after my wedding, María was standing by the front door, waiting for us, dressed in black and looking very solemn. She greeted Howard with a slight nod of her head. When he held out his hand to her, she did not know what to do but took it very slowly then withdrew her hand, and looking him straight in the eye, said, "Take care of her. She's my little girl." Then she took our coats and disappeared.

"Children don't understand the first thing about age. For them, whether one is forty or eighty it's all one and the same, a disaster" (Erri de Luca, *Montedidio*).

* * *

We leave my sister's house. Closing the door behind me I feel I desperately need to take plenty of deep breaths of fresh air. We walk along in silence. Just like us, the Plaza Francia is all quiet and secretive. I would have liked to walk until I dropped but more particularly until I was too tired to think any more. We climb into a taxi and within minutes we are back at the hotel. Although it is nearby, I am afraid to walk in the street late at night. The trauma of the *desaparecidos* (people who disappeared under the military dictatorship) is still there, in the streets of Buenos Aires. So many people were "stolen" off the streets, bundled into cars and never seen again. But sometimes families were "lucky" and bodies resurfaced from the bottom of the River Plate. Thousands of people had no tomb upon which to inscribe their names. The *madres* and *abuelas* (mothers and grandmothers) of the Plaza de Mayo still demonstrate outside the Casa Rosada every Thursday, holding placards and photographs. They wear headscarves, their faces are lined and their eyes red from constant weeping. Their hands clench with pain and anger at a government that betrayed its people, leaving a legacy of distrust. When they can no longer march to the Casa Rosada and are no longer on this earth, then the next generation will take up those placards and photographs and continue with the same march so that the betrayed society never forgets lest it commit the same crime again.

The hotel lobby is quiet. From a radio in the office behind the reception desk come the honeyed tones of some bolero music playing softly. The concierge's eyes are red from lack of sleep.

"Lara, ask them for a wake-up call, please."

"For what time, Mommy?" Noemia is almost asleep on her feet.

"I think we'd better have breakfast at the airport to be on the safe side. Do you think five o'clock would be all right? No, let's say 4:30 because we'll all want to have a shower and half an hour earlier would be better. We'll sleep on the plane."

But none of them is listening. They don't say a word.

There is no reply. Lara goes up to the concierge and asks for the wake-up call.

"Ah, that's good, everything's ready now, isn't it."

All three of them just nod their heads and look at one another as though to say, "Mommy wants to know that we appreciate her organized mind."

It's all right. I understand. I answer them with my "look," as they call it. They say I can make a brick wall tumble down with one of those looks.

* * *

"What did I do, Mamá? Why is Papá looking at me like that?"

"Child, you shouldn't interrupt your father when he's talking, or anyone else. It's bad manners. You must wait your turn."

"But it's never my turn, everyone forgets about me just because I'm the youngest."

"No, Gabriela, you have to learn how to put forward your ideas. If you start telling a long story that goes on forever, my love, no one is patient enough to listen to you. First try to think very carefully about what you want to say before you start talking."

I paid attention to my mother's advice. I listened to her and I learned.

I looked at the wall and it seemed to have a new crack. That was what we children used to say when Papá was annoyed—the wall is cracking.

And now I seem to have that power.

My elementary school was like a house with halls and large courtyards. The classrooms were big with high ceilings. In winter there was a paraffin stove that gave off an unpleasant smell. We sat in pairs and wore uniforms. In the afternoons there was a break from lessons and they would give us hot milk to drink. They would put it on the table in an aluminum jug without a lid and you could see the steam rising from it. It seemed to me like a very important task to carry that jug. My father was a metallurgist and his factory produced jugs, saucepans, toys, and many other things. The milk always had a skin on it, which I hated. Each class had its own jug but they were all identical. Students had to bring *toddy*, powdered sugar, and a biscuit from home.

There are things I still don't understand. Why didn't I have any *toddy*? That chocolate powder that smelled so good as it dissolved, almost as good as the smell I used to imagine whenever I saw an advertisement for chocolate. It made me so happy when a friend— and I didn't have many friends— would give me a small spoonful of *toddy*. Otherwise, I just drank the hot milk plain. I would sit next to Susana Pilar, the daughter of a police superintendent. Her mother had died when she was very small. Susana would arrive at school in a police car. Sometimes, on her way, she would pick me up from home. My parents knew her family and yet they seldom spoke of her father. At that time, being in the police force and in a high position like Susana's father was not a good reference to have. When her father was also in the car, he would sit next to the driver. He spoke very little. I can remember his olive skin, very straight nose, and thin lips. His eyes were always hidden by the visor of his uniform cap. Just thinking of him made me shiver.

Susana and I took the entrance exams for high school together, but then we were put into different courses. It was the Perón regime that separated us. She had been my most loyal friend but then she began to watch me out of the corner of her eye.

Paris

"Let's go to Passy first. The new Kookaï shop has some pretty things. They have their spring collection in," Noemia says.

Noemia loves looking at fashion magazines. Lara and Ayala always ask her advice. She has a natural sense of aesthetics and color and even her school friends copy the way she dresses. But she doesn't see herself like that. She's shy and later on she found it very difficult to accept the fact that they voted her "queen." In Israeli schools there is a custom, sometimes difficult to accept, of naming someone "queen" of the class. It doesn't depend on who's the most clever or the prettiest, but rather who performs the most daring pranks. Almost up to the end of her studies Noemia was never named "queen." She didn't behave badly, she didn't talk back to teachers, and she always showed respect for others. It was no use for all of us to tell her how beautiful, intelligent, and kind she was. She didn't believe us. She felt unimportant. She said to me, "Mommy, I'm the daughter sandwiched between the other two. I can't find my role or my place in this family."

The smart district of Paris, where mothers and daughters can walk around safely and go shopping, is the sixteenth arrondissement, which in a way is the Barrio Norte of Buenos Aires.

My daughters Lara and Noemia came back from school. Ayala was in England, at a private special school for children with learning difficulties.

The school bus dropped them off at the Place Trocadéro. They walked along together. Security was very tight at the Israeli school. There was a lot of tension. Terrorism had come to France and many other parts of Europe. It was the 1980s. The bomb in the rue Copernic Synagogue, the explosion in the Jewish restaurant in the heart of the Marais district, the assassination of an Israeli diplomat in front of his wife— the list was long and dreadfully sad. It was the same on the other side of the Atlantic with very serious attacks against Jewish organizations and property. The perpetrators were hidden by a tangle of complicities and impunity and teams of very clever defense lawyers.

We lived in the sixteenth arrondissement. It was a little too bourgeois for my taste; what the French call "BCBG" (*bon chic, bon genre*). The street we lived on was the rue de Longchamp. For Lara, Noemia, and Ayala it was a dream area for shopping! There was everything and they loved it all. Their tastes were developing and the Paris shop windows spoke a different language from those in Jerusalem when it came to clothes. The girls appreciated the elegance of the styles and they discovered European sophistication. Noemia loved trying out different colors of makeup and Ayala copied her while Lara looked on and laughed.

"How do I look?" Noemia asked, her eyes shining, with quantities of blue eye shadow and blush on her cheeks.

I looked at her and saw behind her Ayala's young face just like a little clown! The saleswoman and I couldn't stop ourselves from laughing. The bells of the church nearby told us it was time to go home.

Just a few blocks away was the Metro, the Place Trocadéro, and the Musée de l'homme. It made a perfect short walk for us with Robin, our dog. She was born in Jerusalem, our desert dog. Her arrival in Paris and on our street caused quite a stir. Robin would greet everyone and, of course, went up to all the elegant, perfumed Parisian dogs. They would look her over and sniff her and then go on their way. She seemed to love it. She knew our walk and its little rituals. Slightly farther on was Passy. Paradise! There was "our" Japanese restaurant with its excellent sushi, which we ate as a treat some weekends. We used to take the car to the Bois de Boulogne on Sundays.

When it was very cold or snowing, the lake would ice over and become a skating rink. One could picture Marcel Proust walking along with his stick and his hat, on the way to the Bagatelle teahouse.

I put the teapot, the milk, and the plates on the kitchen table and got ready to make pancakes with the grated gruyère cheese they like so much. The smell of hot batter, the cheese gradually going golden brown, and the light of the winter afternoon drew us together around our wooden kitchen table. It was a very old table that traveled with us wherever we went. We had our own private world. Both girls were chatting away at the same time. Noemia gave her seat to Lara. The girl with the gentle eyes was listening to her elder sister with respect and, I would even say, admiration.

* * *

Ayala was in England, at school. She came home every three weeks. When she was with us, she loved being the center of attention and got to do everything she wanted. She took the dog out for her walk, she chose which cake to buy, which television program to watch, and she always prepared a dance performance with Noemia. They draped themselves in enormous chiffon scarves of all different colors. They rehearsed with their music in the bedroom they shared and didn't let anyone into the room until it was time for their performance. They made tickets and wrote out the program and the living room was turned into a theater. They drew the curtains and we had to be there on time. Late arrivals weren't allowed in.

How we loved those afternoons with my two little ballerinas! We would clap and they curtsied.

Noemia went to ballet classes for several years. One of her teachers was a baroness who had a small white poodle named Mozart. The baroness was like a character out of a Balzac novel. She had a very wrinkled face with makeup in different shades of pink and dark blue eye shadow. Her clothes were from the nineteenth century and her piercing voice could be heard from the street below in the summer when the windows were open. It was always Ayala's dream to take ballet like Noemia. Although she never did go to ballet classes, she was really good at salsa and rock 'n roll.

When she was seven, Ayala learned how to travel alone, by plane.

I would see her arrive at the airport, in her blue coat and matching hat, with the card slung around her neck that read "UM" to indicate that she was an unaccompanied minor. Her worried eyes would look for us. A flight attendant stayed with her until we got there. Even today, she still has the manners of a girl educated at boarding school. I don't know how to explain it. It's the way she drinks her tea, the way she eats, and her reserved behavior. Her world was those schools and the school friends she trusted to whom she would tell her secrets. I would say they were almost her family. They were the ones who saw her wake up, laugh, cry, and fall in love. Not us. That separation, which was so painful to us, was what helped her progress; it formed her character, her independence, and it helped her overcome her initial problems.

* * *

"Ooh! It's burning! Careful!"

"I like it burned," said Noemia.

"You got back early from the office, Mommy, what a surprise!" Lara said, looking at me questioningly while she took her place at the head of the table in the small, warm kitchen in the late autumn afternoon.

"Well, you see I missed you and wanted to be here to give you your tea."

The warmth and togetherness is engraved in my memory and comes back to me at the most unexpected moments, particularly when I'm feeling depressed. They are my capital, my fortress against doubts and confusion.

I certainly don't want to criticize my mother, but when I was a child I didn't have that kind of warmth and togetherness. And yet I do remember once or twice when I hoped for tea or something special that was for me and no one else. I also remember the temper tantrums I used to throw as a spoiled child and my hurtful words. My mother was no great cook but sometimes she would try to give us a little something special that children and husbands expect.

One Friday, it was in the winter, during a vacation from school. In my memory, those were wonderful days without school. I could just stay at home and read, sitting in front of the fire, dreaming.

My mother was trying to make a cake. She called me and said, "Look, Gabrielita, my cake for tonight." My mother held out the plate to me. She proudly showed it to me. She was wearing an apron so as not to get her clothes dirty. Her fingernails were full of flour and there was some on one of her cheeks, making her look funny—something rare with her. She had a big smile on her face and her hair was a little messy because of the heat of the kitchen. She was waiting for me to praise her efforts.

Does a mother need admiration and praise from her children?

It seems they do. But aren't they on a pedestal, placed there by us, the children? Isn't that why they are superior, protected, and far removed from the husband's and the children's everyday problems?

"But, Má, it's flat. It hasn't risen. That's not a cake. It looks like a very brown, almost burned pancake."

My mother left the kitchen in tears.

Doña María, the cook, is looking at me angrily. She says, "You don't talk to your mother like that! Go and apologize immediately! You're impossible!"

They punished me for being rude.

It took a long time for me to be able to look my mother in the eye, and even longer for me to understand how hurt she was.

There was much sorrow and pain that I only came to understand far later.

* * *

My daughters decided that each night one of them would sleep in my room. Tonight it's Ayala's turn.

"I'll go and take a shower first, if…" I begin, but then I see she's already fallen asleep. She's holding the blue book that is going to be the diary of our journey through her eyes. I take it from her, trying not to wake her. Her lips are slightly parted. I touch her silky black hair. I want to give her a kiss and hug her to make up for all those other nights when I didn't see her sleeping, when I didn't listen to her about her dreams, when I didn't cover her up again if she'd shrugged off the blankets.

Can we get the past back and make up for our mistakes? That's what I'm trying to do on this journey: a search for Gabriela and where I am now and why. Well, at least the worst is over—the first meeting with Dora.

I close the bathroom door and turn on the shower. It does me good.

I'm trying hard for there not to be such a barrier between my daughters and me. Do I lean on them too much, making them take part in both the good and the bad aspects of married life? Do I really see them as daughters or as friends? Where is the dividing line?

I think I'm putting on weight.

I look at myself in the big bathroom mirror and realize I need to go to the gym. Dieting just isn't enough. I tend to get a tummy like my mother had. When I was small, I used to love massaging her tummy with talc. She seemed to really enjoy it too. A moment of extreme intimacy. Perhaps unique.

"Mommy, can I come in?" It's Ayala's voice.

"Of course you can. What's wrong? Can't you sleep?"

She sits on the toilet and relieves herself of gallons of liquid.

"Doesn't that feel great, Mommy?"

"Yes, Ayala, and your tummy goes down and so does your weight."

She flushes the toilet, washes her hands, and looks at my reflection in the mirror.

"Mommy, why don't you love your sister?"

Typical Ayala. Straight to the point with very few words. Although she only began to talk when she was four, she knows how to use exactly the right words.

"I don't know how to answer you, really. Let's talk about it another time. I'm finished with the bathroom. Let's try to sleep now."

I dry myself and open a pot of body cream. How strange, I'm not ashamed of my body in front of my daughters. I'm beginning to get veins in my calves, just like my father. What should I do to prevent them from getting any worse?

* * *

"Keep still, Gabriela!"

I was in the bath. My sister Dora had decided to bathe me. María had gone out. I wanted to take a bath on my own.

"Keep still, Gabriela!"

Dora picked up the sponge, one of those hard, light-colored sponges. It looked like boiled chicken. She scrubbed me. She held my shoulder and rubbed the sponge hard over my skin. I could feel her tense breath on me. She was muttering "Dirt, we've got to get rid of the dirt."

What dirt was she talking about? Hers or mine?

It was the summer when I was sixteen. I met Federico and his entire family who, like us, were taking a vacation by the sea. I saw him from a distance but near enough to see he was really tall, suntanned, and above all the blueness of his eyes. They were so dark they looked almost black. His parents were from Poland. They were all very different from my family.

I played on the beach with a bat and ball. I was very good at it and my sisters knew that it wasn't easy to play with me. I played with my brother Arielito. It was different with him.

Federico came up to me and suggested we play a game together. For the rest of the summer we played, talked, and laughed a lot. He wasn't my boyfriend or what was termed "boyfriend" back then. He was my "entertainer." That's how Doña María, our cook, referred to him.

My parents didn't like him. My mother had very rigid rules about who could or couldn't talk to her daughters.

Federico read a lot. He knew about so many things of which I was totally unaware. We were the same age and we were both conscious of my parents' disapproval.

One morning, in response to something my sister, Adela, said, I talked back. My mother sent me up to the house. I was perfectly happy to go back but I felt humiliated. I didn't think of myself as a child anymore. Back at the house I had some tea and began reading. I closed the door of my room so as to enjoy being alone all the more. I wanted them to see that it didn't matter to me. Later on, the maid called me. Young Federico was in the hall and wanted to see me.

He hugged me but didn't kiss me. When we stood apart I understood for the first time what an erection was.

Before leaving to go back to Buenos Aires, he gave me a letter. It was my first love letter. It was dreadfully emotional. I hid it. I didn't want anyone else to see it. I read it I don't know how many times. I analyzed it with cold curiosity as though it wasn't addressed to me. I wanted to understand who he was talking about. I stepped away from the other person without knowing who she was. I looked at myself in the mirror hoping to find an answer there. I touched my face to try to understand what was happening.

I saw him again in the city when a group of us went out together for a Coca-Cola. We listened to gentle music and danced the "slow." We went to one of those places that opened in the afternoons for well-behaved young people to meet there and perhaps things would develop into more formal relations. Or perhaps they would do everything or almost everything they weren't allowed to do. The actual district where this sort of encounter developed indicated to which level the relationship had progressed. In the Barrio Norte, things were completely innocent. If the boy already had a car, then that was a very big plus. With a car they were able to discover each other's bodies and feelings, then they would arrive home with swollen lips. Farther away from the city center, in districts like Vicente Lopez, Martínez, and Olivos, there were already nightclubs where you couldn't go until you were old enough.

Meeting someone again after a while, even if it was only a short span of time, but in a totally different atmosphere from that of the beach, the sun, vacation clothes, and suntans, there was a certain awkwardness at first. Federico's blue eyes were even bluer, his suntan made him look healthy, and also he seemed more mature. With his white shirt, gray pants, and blue blazer he seemed older and more sophisticated than when he'd worn shorts, a T-shirt, and sandals on the beach. It was difficult to move closer together. We looked at each other rather like animals do when they sniff to see if they recognize the other one. Yes, we recognized each other and stepped closer. It was my curiosity about discovering something new that attracted me to him sexually rather than mentally.

The strict life of a conservative, almost Victorian society made our thoughts veer toward what was forbidden—although not written down as such but implied.

I had to be home by nine in the evening. My sister Juana acted as my chaperone. How absurd all those rules were and yet we abided by them because that was the way it was for young people—at least those in our social class.

I remember the dress I wore that day. It was white cotton piqué. Federico's cousin spilled her glass of Coca-Cola on my dress. I looked at her, very surprised. She stared back at me in a strange way. I didn't understand. When I danced with Federico I could feel him very close to me. His breath on my cheek excited me. He gave me a present of the smallest bottle of perfume I had ever seen. I didn't open it. I hid it among my clothes.

It all finished in May. I was bored. So much adolescent passion wasn't what I wanted. If at least he'd played a good game of tennis, but he didn't.

Three more months went by until he kissed me. We were on our way home from school.

Two months later I broke up with him. My father forbade me to continue seeing him.

I don't know when or how I decided that this wasn't what I wanted. Everything around me seemed to be happening in a sort of airless, dark, gray cloud.

I saw him again many years later, in Jerusalem, where we were both studying. When we looked at each other we were seized with the same thought. Was it just chance there was still that electricity between us?

We started seeing each other. One Saturday he took me to see Herod's tomb and the border between Israel and Jordan. It was when Jerusalem was very peaceful and still divided. We climbed up to the summit of Mount Zion and looked toward what we were to discover many years later: Salah Adin, the main street of Old Jerusalem. From the height of Notre Dame or Mount Zion, we could see a mysterious, unknown world. We felt drawn to that forbidden world. Jordanian soldiers often opened fire toward our part of Jerusalem. The writing of grief that wars leave behind them is still even today etched into the walls of the former Barclays Bank on the corner of Jaffa Street where the dividing wall used to be. In August 1967, we walked along, touching those stones and felt we had returned home.

As for the Western Wall, it continues to receive pleas between the cracks and crevices of its stones that beat—as tradition has it—in the presence of the humble who know how to listen.

"Your great-grandmother Golda took the boat from Odessa. She arrived in Palestine and traveled to Jerusalem on a donkey. She wanted to die in the Holy Land. Her husband, Yona, was with her. Neither of them died. They came back to Europe. Then time went by. Many years passed. In the end, your great-grandfather died first and he's buried in Jaffa. She died two years later. She's buried in Jerusalem." My father used to tell this story with many variations.

Just at that time, after the Six-Day War, my father, Nathan, sent me a letter with the names of all our ancestors who were buried in Jerusalem. I found the graves. They had been destroyed. My grandfather David wasn't able to return to Jerusalem. The Germans took care of that. He was a strong Zionist who saw that the future of the Jewish people lay in this land.

"Gabriela, for your mother and me it was always our dream to go back to our roots, though I know that's not going to be possible now. But you can. Think about it."

It didn't take me more than five minutes to think about it.

"Pá, you know I ran away from all the Jewish schools in Buenos Aires and I've never managed to learn Hebrew and I'm interested in politics. How would I be able to study there? Yes, I'd love to go, but how…"

"Don't you worry about it, I'll call the Embassy and we'll talk to the Counselor…"

"But what will Mamá say?"

I began to wake up. I asked questions, I asked myself what I was thinking, I became another person, someone who would feel loneliness and discover a new world.

It was when Argentina was suffering through wretched times, with the military in power. The third generation of our family joined the guerrillas fighting against the Junta. Three of my cousins died, two while in prison. Others left the country, which seemed to hold no future for them and certainly offered no security. I lost touch with those who left. It was very sad.

* * *

We arrive at the synagogue to hear voices receiving the blessing for Shabbat. We had left the north and are back in the city again.

The rabbi looks at us. His eyes briefly leave the prayer book and he receives us with his glance. His wife has kept seats for us beside her.

It feels so very strange to be here with my daughters. I try not to look at the door. We have arranged with my sister that we will meet here.

I can feel she is there before I see her. I look up and there she is. She seems annoyed. We make room for her to sit with us. She kisses me coldly. My daughters are reserved. I understand that they don't know how to behave around her. How do they see all this? Is it so very different from the world in which they live?

But what am I saying? Am I afraid they're going to judge the place where I was born and grew up? That they're going to assess whether or not I'm a reflection of that society? Will I be me? The mother in Paris or Jerusalem? Or that other person, the one I left behind here over thirty years ago? Will I be loyal to them or to my past? And if it's not for all those unanswered questions, then what am I doing here?

* * *

"Adela, can I have a word with you?" I was almost ready to leave for the boat. It was the day I was leaving for Israel. I had decided to study at the Hebrew University of Jerusalem. I had talked it over with my father and he understood that I felt stifled by life in Buenos Aires. I did not get on well with the rest of the family and I wanted to travel. My parents accepted my decision on the condition that I would travel in order to study.

"What do you want?" the second of my three sisters, Adela, responded.

"This is my diary. Will you please destroy it for me when I leave? I can't bring myself to do it."

"I promise I'll do it. Don't worry."

Years later, she quoted back to me whole sentences and feelings I'd confided to my diary in those most secret moments of my adolescence and she had joked about them with my other sisters and their girlfriends.

How do I see all that now? Was I partly to blame for so much discord? Perhaps some of it was my fault. I must find answers in order to be able to look at myself, there may be other ways, but at least now the best approach is to confront it.

Yes, we all harbor grudges and bad memories. Confronting them is hard but I want to do it. That's why I'm on this journey of reconciliation. I don't want to call it one of forgiveness or reproach. Nor do I want these words to become a bitter list of grievances. I want to know *the I and the thou*. There is still a long way to go.

On a Friday, in March — it was 1964, the year I'd left home—I found a letter waiting for me when I got back to my dorm room in

Jerusalem. My mother wrote that my father had become very upset during the kiddush and broke down in tears. My father cried? Perhaps they love me after all.

I went and studied Hebrew and I think I must have been the worst student. It didn't interest me. I walked and walked along the narrow streets of Jerusalem. I drank very hot tea served in a glass in the bakeries of Mea Shearim, the Orthodox district, where they sold cheesecake and yeast and cinnamon rolls. I had never tried them before. I loved them and I still do. On Thursday nights, the predominant color of that district was the black of the men's beards and large hats. The men adopted that style of dress worn in Poland and other Eastern European countries more than two hundred years ago. They still dress that way today despite the fact that it is totally ill-suited to the torrid, dry Israeli summer. The women wear wigs from the day they marry. Very often, that day is the first time they see their husband-to-be.

I would stop to look inside the apartments, especially when night fell and the lights were on inside. There were always bookcases crammed with books of different sizes. Some looked as though they were about to topple off the shelves; some were very worn. If I stayed watching for a while I could see the man of the house—or the person I took to be the man of the house—go to the bookshelves, look for the book he wanted, find it, lower his glasses halfway down his nose, give a hint of a smile, and turn around very slowly, placing a finger on the text as though caressing it. These men all wore a *kippa* (yarmulke).

I expect most of the books were religious texts, commentaries on the sacred books or perhaps in many cases they were philosophy books. I also often saw the woman of the house. She would be quietly looking for something. Sometimes she would come into the room with a glass of tea for her husband.

I had to force myself to move away. I was afraid they would see me or that someone would ask what that young woman was doing standing there, looking through the window. The privacy from the inside seeped through to the outside world.

I will never understand those people. They seem to be locked away in a different world and in a different time.

The window opened a door for me and I silently went in.

I absorbed everything. I was invisible. I could go from room to room and no one would see me. I opened and closed doors, tasted the food in the cooking pots, smelled the sheets in the cupboards, listened to the gentle words of a mother to her children, saw the look of love the man gave the woman. It was not true that there was no passion. They didn't show it in public; it was private and very secret. The Orthodox woman could acquire a deal of power. Looking after the home, the children, and the household finances were all in her hands. Many of the women studied, ran businesses, and gained respect. Others lived in times past. I could not, nor did I want, to judge them. I listened to them talking on the bus on my way back from university. There was such understanding among them. Their lives were organized. They knew the rules and abided by them.

I wondered whether they were really content with so many rules. Did they have freedom of choice, could they show their love, could they go out into the world around them? They only saw it through a bus window, or shopping, or in airports. No, I couldn't understand it. I wanted to get to know them properly. My plan was to start talking and get into conversation with them. I must not judge them on the basis of so little knowledge.

I had no rules. I had freedom. It was what I came looking for; what I was seeking. And yet, a very small voice reminded me of commentaries, sayings, and rules. My mother's voice came to me at the most unexpected moments. I saw my father's strict look through a mist of doubts.

My parents had an arranged marriage. They were introduced to each other at my grandparents' house on November 13. One week later my father asked for my mother's hand and a week after that they became engaged. They were married early the following year. They were together for forty-seven years and had six children. One baby girl lived for only nine months. I'm the last child, the unexpected one. Time and again I was reminded of that over the years, even now.

During the seven days of mourning, according to Jewish tradition, after my father's death, I read my mother's diary, which was bound in dark brown velvet. It had notes she had written at that time and I learned a lot about them both, their love, the passion that united them, their clash of personalities, the differences that separated them and attracted one to the other, and also their friendship.

On the evening of the seventh day, the rabbi came to read a prayer and thus close our week of reflection. Only after thirty days can one visit the cemetery and after eleven months the gravestone is put in place. Everything was carried out according to Orthodox rules. My mother said that's how Papá would have wanted it.

I can remember I must have been about six when my father received the news that his father, Moshe Goldemberg, had died before the Germans entered the city. The letter said that he had decided to die. He wanted to be buried according to Jewish tradition. He let himself die; they were able to bury him and put up the stone with his name on it.

Papá sat on the patio on a very low chair and placed stones around him. He wore a white, collarless shirt, slippers, and a *kippa*. He read and prayed for a long time.

Later, the rabbi came and made him get up from the low chair. My father's eyes were very red. My mother went to him and hugged him, murmuring comforting words of love.

It was seven years later that my father learned of the exact date of his father's death. He didn't know until then that he still had relatives who had lived through the war and survived the concentration camps. He didn't know that his elder brother Motke and his wife, before arriving in Israel, had been interned in the British camps in Cyprus.

All their children were there to meet them when they came off the boat, their clothes in tatters. One son had been a partisan, another had fought in Israel's War of Independence, and their daughters had been working on kibbutzim. They were able to see grandchildren they didn't even know had been born.

When my mother left the house for the first time after my father's death and the seven days of mourning, I went with her to the hairdresser. I understood that it was her way of saying to her husband, "I'm listening to you, you want me to stay strong even though you're not here anymore." On the way home we walked through the Plaza Francia across from our house. My father used to love sitting on the balcony, looking at the activity in the square, a cup of *maté* in his hand and commenting on the trees, the dogs and their masters, and the children playing. Turning onto the Calle Quintana, we met one of my mother's acquaintances. Like my mother, she was dressed elegantly, wearing gloves, and not a hair moved in her exaggerated hairstyle. I remember she spoke very bad Spanish.

"Doña Perla, how are you?"

They addressed each other formally. That generation did not use the familiar Spanish *tu* with one another but kept their distance whether they were speaking Spanish or Yiddish.

"How am I?" my mother responded, looking at the woman but not really seeing her. Her eyes were dull, her voice hoarse as though she hadn't spoken for a long time. Then almost immediately she said in Yiddish, "*Mein mann ist toit!*" (My husband is dead.)

It was a cry but so soft that only the three of us could hear it.

I had the sensation that the sky had become clouded over and there seemed to be a cold gust of wind enveloping us, although it was the hot month of November, spring in the southern hemisphere. I shivered.

"I'm sorry. I didn't know. I only just returned from the country," her friend apologized, not knowing what else to say.

Mamá walked on. I was holding her arm. I was afraid she might fall. I suddenly felt how fragile and defenseless she was. Papá wasn't there anymore to protect her. My mother would have to find inner strength. When we got home I made a cup of tea for her. I took it to her sitting room, the one we used to call the blue sitting room, where she and Papá used to play chess.

"Má, your lime flower tea."

"Natán, where are you?" she cried out like a wounded animal. Is this really my mother? I didn't seem to know this woman sitting in front of me; she had always seemed so brusque and distant and never spoke of love for her husband or anyone else. I looked over toward the windows hoping for something; perhaps my father was there and would answer her. They were together for such a long time and loved one another so much. She expressed all of that in those few words.

My mother's face became calm again. She drank the tea and asked me to read her something. I remember she said "please" that one time.

"Today we went to the theater with Natán and my parents. He brought me a box of sweets. He's so different from the other men with whom I've gone out. He's very European, so shy and very good-looking..."

I looked at Mamá to see if she wanted me to go on reading. Her green eyes were shining and she was almost smiling.

"Gabrielita, I never told your father how much I loved him. Don't make the same mistake. Say what you feel."

I listened to those words of hers and I have followed her advice.

> Each person in proportion to his ignorance inflicts great ills upon himself and other members of his species. If men were wise, they would not harm one another, and because knowledge of the truth moves away from hatred and quarrels thus deterring mutual wrongs.
>
> *Maimonides*

"Do you think they're all going to come? Or am I going to be left high and dry?" I asked my third sister, Juana, while she helped me put my hair in a ponytail. It was my favorite hairstyle but I couldn't manage to do it on my own.

In the mirror I could see her green eyes. They seemed almost gentle.

"Of course they'll come and they'll give you wonderful birthday presents. Now don't move or I won't be able to fix the hairband and it'll all fall down."

It was hot. We didn't go away for vacation this year. Juana helped me prepare for my birthday party. Doña María made me a pretty cake with glacé icing and cream. There were colored napkins on the table and everything was already prepared for the hot chocolate we'd have at four o'clock. In two small bowls we stuck daisies in some sand we'd taken from the building site next to our house. The white plates were laid out on the white tablecloth. It all seemed fresh as though the table were set in a garden. The curtains were drawn to keep out the heat of the day. I looked at everything and felt satisfied with our handiwork. Juana really seemed to have understood my need to feel special.

"I'm going to have a bath," she said. "You'd better change now. The guests will start arriving soon."

I looked admiringly at my dress. It was beautiful. It was a sailor style with blue and white stripes. The colors were so fresh and matched my hairband. I polished my white moccasins until they were shiny. My ankle socks and underwear were all pretty and scented. I looked at my reflection in the mirror and wondered if I'd changed. Did I look more like a señorita? I hadn't had my first period yet. My breasts were small. I undid the top of my dress and looked at them. Would they get bigger? Mamá said they would. I hoped she was right. But actually I wouldn't like them to be heavy like some girls at school who wear bodices like old women wear. I didn't like my nose. They told me I had a Greek profile but I thought my nose was enormous. I thought my eyes were my face's best feature. Maybe they were a bit sad but they changed color depending on the light and my moods. Juana used to say they were the color of diarrhea.

"Are you there?"

The door opened and there are my parents.

"But, but...what a surprise!"

"Did you think we weren't going to be with you for your birthday? You're our little one."

They hugged and kissed me. I smelled their scent like a cub trying to recognize its family. There was my mother's scent mingled with the smell of my father's tobacco. They were hot with a slight film of perspiration. Their breath was warm, very warm and sweet. Their bodies were tense with excitement.

I thought perhaps they might have forgotten as they'd been away for a few days but there they were. They were both laughing like teenagers, happy to have given me such a surprise.

I looked back at my mother and smiled. I wanted to convey to her how I felt in that moment, the color of our laughter and the fragrance of our happiness on that hot, magic February day.

That day, Má, you were wearing that blue linen sundress with a low-cut back showing your soft, white skin of which you were so proud. We all heard when Papá would say to you, "Perlita, you have such soft skin." And then you would laugh with that sound of crystal bells. Now I understand the flirtatiousness and not giving in easily to a man.

I don't think I understood very much. I was in admiration of them just as one admires movie stars. I had a strong feeling that they belonged to me and that made me feel proud but it didn't make me feel safe. I was afraid of the jealous fights they had. When you preferred your educated, aristocratic side of the family, Má, as you considered yourselves to be, I would side with my father. I wanted to protect him. I didn't understand then how special your family was. They all seemed to me to be rather vague, conceited, and terribly boring. I think my grandmother—the only one I ever knew—did like Papá very much. But perhaps it was respect more than affection. I made a promise to myself that I would never do that, but rather I would respect my husband's family. What I never understood was how you spoke to us with pride of Papá's family but were disrespectful about them in front of your brothers and sisters. It was so painful to see Pá's face on those occasions. He would distance himself from the group and listen to their discussions on

Tolstoy and all the others. No one ever asked him anything or tried to include him in their philosophical discussions. Mamá, I think it hurt you to see him so ignored.

For a child, understanding that one's parents are a couple and have their own relationship can help forge one's future. Seeing them as the man and the woman they then were allows us to compare our own adult relationships and ask questions not as children any more, but as adults.

But in order to establish that distance and reach a reasonable analysis, I must free myself of my own doubts and complexes. The fact that they arrived so unexpectedly that hot February Sunday made me sit up and take notice. That couple whose skin shone with sex and energy made me see my parents in a totally new light.

* * *

That is all coming back to me now on this journey with my daughters. It is the path I am taking to reencounter the land where I was born; images come back to me that blind me from the past, images previously unknown to me. We find ourselves repeating the same gestures and words and inflicting the same blows on others just like when we ourselves were on the receiving end.

* * *

It is not easy being the youngest of six children, at least not without clashing with the others. You have to fight for your basic rights like giving your opinion on things, talking during meals without being interrupted and usually not being listened to. You have to stand up for yourself so that you're not sent off to do things for the others because there's no way to respond to their continual claim that you're the youngest so it's up to you to do whatever it is they want done. Clothes are never new but always passed down from the older ones. Camel hair coats and velvet dresses never seem to wear out. And when I protested and asked why, the answer was always the same: "That's how it should be. We're not nouveaux riches."

When I was ten I insisted on having my own newspaper and I wanted it to be an English one. My father agreed to my demand. That was a battle well won. Another prestigious victory was when I was allowed to have my very own brand new tennis racket. It was expensive. I can still remember how, when, and where I chose it. It was a Wilson. I ordered it from a sports shop on the Avenida Callao. It's a street where even today some parts retain a French, or more specifically Parisian, style. When I walk along the Avenue Victor Hugo in Paris I can see there are striking similarities with the Avenida Callao in Buenos Aires. Even the smells are similar. In Paris, it's the smell of the early morning croissants in the *boulangeries* that entice us and in Buenos Aires the *panaderías* tempt us with their buttery *medialunas*.

I felt very important. I was someone with the right to decide about paying out such an enormous sum of money on something for myself. When the racket arrived and I went back to the shop to pick it up, that was a day of celebration. The racket had its own red and white checked cover and the tennis balls were in their separate box and there was even a matching wristband. I didn't wear tennis shorts; instead I had a dress I loved wearing when I played tennis. I was getting ready for each change and every step was taking me toward freedom. I was gently testing the ground although not yet bringing about an actual revolution. I stored up each moment whether good or bad and learned from them. That hoard of experience was something I could keep and take out whenever I needed to call on it. I was building my pyramid.

When I finished school I wanted to go to the department of philosophy. My sister Dora objected. She convinced my parents it was a place full of revolutionaries and so I couldn't go. It became a lost year for me. My father suggested I work in his office at the factory. That was when I finally understood that Buenos Aires wasn't big enough for me and I had to find my way out.

It was still the Perón government back then. The so-called "liberating revolution" was yet to come. General Aramburu and his followers were readying themselves in Córdoba while Perón's radio broadcasts said, "They're cleaning up Córdoba." Córdoba became the symbol from where, once again, the voice of freedom was born, which in some way seemed to me to be linked with its university and history—the seat of learning founded by the Jesuits in 1613, just fourteen years after their arrival in the region. Córdoba is the oldest university in South America.

Going back. I made many mistakes and I know I ran away. I must not be ashamed. I must open my eyes and once again, smell the pizzas in the Calle Corrientes, see them spread out like great fans. It's like looking and waking up to open the window. It's like saying to people passing by, "You came outside to look at the sky, the street, and the color. But I'm here, I've arrived in these streets with their cracked tiles. I'm not criticizing. I'm looking for my footprints that have been erased by so many others. I'm exhausted and my mouth is dry. I'm looking for the water of my childhood."

I don't know whether my face is wet with the gray rain of Buenos Aires or with my tears falling unashamedly.

*   *   *

There was much sorrow and pain that I only came to understand a great while later.

My father left home when he was twenty. He hadn't seen his parents since. Sometimes he would gaze into space, looking at something far away where no one could go and that no one knew. He was looking for something. Perhaps he was afraid of forgetting their faces or his past or of not remembering them anymore. If that happened, they would be dead forever.

Now, forty years later, I'm going to carry out one of his wishes: I'm going to say the prayer for the dead over his parents' graves. My husband has encouraged us to make this journey and overcome the challenges of what he calls "the land of ghosts."

I needed to go back for my father, to where he was born. So often he would tell us of the small Ukrainian town where he grew up. The grove of trees he used to walk through, the Dniester River where he used to swim in the summer in the bright sunshine. I saw the green hills and imagined how they must look in the winter, covered in snow. I saw my father on his sledge, racing down the hillside at top speed, with a fur hat on his head and looking so happy. I saw the land where once the family house stood and I pictured the large fireplace around which it must have felt so good to lie down.

I saw the school he ran away from to play football with his friends; the synagogue where he had his bar mitzvah. I saw everything that isn't there anymore, I saw it through his eyes, eyes that can no longer see. I went to the cemetery to meet ancestors who lived two hundred years ago. I saw the same names over and over again, through the generations. I didn't find my grandparents' graves. There were broken headstones, scattered on the ground. Weeds had sprung up and grown over them, covering them with tangles of vegetation so that at least nature hid the shame from the sadness. Desecrated, violated graves. Graves that were never witness to those who said Kaddish in memory of the dead.

The faces around me were expecting me to cry. I couldn't. It wasn't intentional. I simply couldn't. I listened to the words of my father's stories. I wanted, I hoped I would see him running quickly by, his hair flying in the wind, and his eyes would meet mine and say "Gabrielita, that was me, do you recognize me?"

That man so full of ideas of freedom and with such a love of life had neither fears nor complexes. He left for America and conquered it. He integrated into the new society and built a new life for himself. He looked back, yes, but only to draw strength from the past to help him keep going forward.

Roots and Ruins: Stories to be Told

I looked at the ancient Castle of Chotin that weathered battles against the Turks and the Poles who wanted to keep it. I pictured my father as a boy playing soldiers. What side would he have been on? How did they defend themselves in those ancient wars?

What were my aunts like when they went out, strolling along the boulevard, talking with my grandmother? Was she strict but easygoing and smiling? Or just the opposite?

I walked along, looking for footprints, but the rain had washed them all away.

People were looking at me. I know. I was clearly not one of them. Howard was watching me. Was he afraid? Was he waiting for some reaction from me? What did he think I was going to do? Did he think I was going to hammer on the door of that house damaged by fire, war, and bad reconstruction? What for? Was he afraid of the way I might behave in front of today's inhabitants? Why?

We sat down to eat in the shade of sadness. I was thirsty. I wanted to breathe in all the air around me. I wanted this same oxygen that gave life to my father to give strength to me. I needed to understand what had happened, what was lying in wait for me, and to discover who I am. I needed to touch the ashes of barbarity.

The two Romanians accompanying us were smoking and eating. Howard was following their conversation and I was grateful for the lull that left me to indulge in my own silence. The noise of the voices let me listen to my other voices, which were fighting to be heard while in turn I was struggling to understand them.

A draft of air struck me full in the face. But there was no wind. Where was it coming from? So strong I had to close my eyes against it. Where was that white light coming from, filtering through the shade of the shop? I heard a horse trotting along. The rider stopped in front of us. I went up to them. The colt didn't shy away but let me stroke its head. It looked at me and I think it smiled.

Papá loved animals, especially dogs and horses. I smiled at the rider but he didn't return my smile. He wanted money. He understood that I liked the horse but if I wanted a photograph, if I asked his permission for Howard to take a photograph of me with the horse, I would have to pay for it. The poverty that prevailed throughout this region was so tangible it seemed to shout in our faces: *I want to eat, I want to drink, I want to live, pay! Pay! Can't you understand?*

Seeing the cigarette stuck between his dry lips, his torn fingernails and hands covered in sores, we knew how very poor the guide was. His face seemed to mock us; he couldn't hide what he was thinking: What's that well-dressed Jewish woman doing, searching for her grandparents' graves? What are they looking for among the dead? Didn't we persecute them enough? Don't they understand how we hate them and the suspiciousness that these visits reawaken in us? Don't they understand that if they give us a few dollars we'll spend it on vodka, which isn't even vodka but pure alcohol?

Yes, I recognized you. I learned all about you through my father's stories, dear *mujik*, I knew exactly what you were thinking but for the time being you were going to have to put up with me.

I wanted to get away from everything around me, just get up and leave without making any noise. The surroundings of the castle were a mass of tourists, mainly Romanians. It was mostly citizens of countries that were once part of the USSR that travel around Eastern Europe. Traveling through these countries one feels no warmth or friendship and certainly no gratitude but quite the opposite—people show deep-rooted animosity and contempt.

For centuries, all over this region, land and power kept changing hands. Maintaining traditions was one of the strengths of each group's nationalism and pride. The Soviet Union did not manage to get rid of those feelings that are passed on from one generation to the next.

Although everyone had to learn Russian, nowadays they refuse to admit knowing any. Street names were changed over the years to reflect the conqueror of the time—names were Russian, Polish, Romanian, and finally back to their original Ukrainian. My father was born with one nationality but when he left Chotin he held another. The mother of one of my cousins used to say that in her *shtetl* they had changed nationality three times in a single day. Each change brought with it new fears. Most of that part of the family refuse to talk about the suffering of forced emigration. They served the various rulers, they went to war and fought under the banner of whoever the current ruler was, but they always kept their religion and their traditions.

I have photographs of my Uncle Motke in his Austro-Hungarian army uniform. He looks very smart and proud. My grandfather David went and followed him through the various battles, trying to rescue him from enlistment that, although initially for three years, ended up being fifteen. He certainly wasn't the only one. There were many others like him who said they were Jewish, so they were kept in the army until they couldn't take any more and converted. They were never made officers. As far as I know, at least when I was still there, Jews were not admitted to the military academy in Argentina. In order to be considered for some positions in the judicial and legislative bodies, the requirements were to have been born in Argentina and to be a member of the Catholic church.

In Germany, assimilation was the means to become integrated intellectually into German *Kultur*. Young men who fought in the 1870 Franco-Prussian War or the 1914–18 war were grudgingly acknowledged or rewarded for having given their lives in exchange for Europe's greatness.

Many young men mutilated themselves in order to avoid conscription. That is why my father was sent to Argentina.

By coming here, I wanted—although I was aware of the hopelessness of the exercise—to avoid being seen as a typical tourist. I didn't want to shape its past nor did I want to gloss over its present. I only wanted to capture images and rhythms of what they told me, of the whispers of what was unsaid and then shape them into writing so they could be shared.

My husband understood that we needed to leave. We exchanged a few words and walked toward the car. The tourists were still buying souvenirs. Howard bought me a book on the history of Chotin and as he gave it to me he said, "Here, take it, it's partly your story as well."

I have the book here in front of me as I write. But I haven't opened it. I want to hold on to my father's words. To me they seem more authentic, more my own.

We thought perhaps this pilgrimage might help me better understand the silence of my past and my search for the origin of my doubts and maybe it worked, just briefly.

Was this journey of mine the return my father couldn't undertake? Did this journey have any parallel with mine, with the one I began with my daughters? Was I trying to relive the steps my father took so as to understand my own?

He left. He escaped from the hell of a Europe on the brink of destruction and when finally that devastation came about he wasn't there when it took with it all those millions of people.

I didn't escape. I chose to make a journey. A journey to a land that from the very cradle I had been taught was our own true land.

Argentina seems to slip through my fingers and from my memory. And yet it is still so much a part of me. There is so much love and so many sweet memories that I need to accept it, and now I am doing just that, through the eyes of my daughters.

*　*　*

Where are my friends? My father would tell us endless stories about his childhood friends. I try to recall faces and expressions but only a few come back to me.

I can picture my brother's face, my brother with whom I used to go to the movie theater when he came home on the weekend. Weekends were when he spent time with us, when he was back from the various schools where he spent most of his life until he was too old to be at boarding school any more.

I can remember his hand in mine when we would catch the no. 84 tram to take us to the Gaona movie theater.

I take my daughters to that neighborhood. I want to go on that same tram ride with them. The movie theater isn't there anymore. They listen to me. They see me walking along with him, chatting away about when and how we'll buy all the sweets and deciding how much we'll spend. We enjoy laughing because we can do it on our own, without anyone stopping us and saying that so many sweets will harm our teeth. But we love sweets so we don't care!

I can hear his voice and sense his fears.

I can remember watching movies that made a very strong impression on us. The *Prisoner of Zenda* was one of those films and *Scaramouche* was another. We loved them and went to see them all over again. We memorized parts and would retell each other the story in the greatest of detail.

I can remember the Laponia ice cream with its wrapper that we'd be very careful to take off as quietly as possible. We hated the rustling noise of toffee papers in the middle of a movie. And even worse was when that person compounded the offense by chewing noisily! That really irritated us.

"Má, you still have that problem when you go to see a movie with us. You turn around to see who those noisy people are, chewing away…"

"…and with their mouths open!" Lara finishes.

And they start laughing. It does me good. This is the music I need to hear.

I go on telling my story but my voice has changed. It's full of a past that I can finally remember with happiness just for having lived it.

Yes, I can remember the looks the people in the street gave us. They'd look from him to me. I can remember saying in a loud voice, "What are you staring at? Do you see something strange?"

My brother's face, his features those of a young boy with Down's syndrome. He wouldn't say a word but just held my hand even tighter. He felt protected but he could never avoid the looks people would give him. He knew he was different.

Before leaving the house, María would inspect us from head to toe to make sure all was in order. She would look at our fingernails, our shoes, our hair, and then she would lecture us on how we should behave: "Don't talk to strangers, stay together and be careful crossing the road. When the movie is over, you're to come straight home. Don't run, hold yourselves straight, keep your heads up, and don't be afraid."

I remember something that happened many years later. I wasn't living in Buenos Aires anymore but I had gone back there to spend the holidays at my parents' house. I was on my way back from shopping. It was winter and the trees in the Plaza Francia were swaying in the wind. It wasn't that late. The lights of the shops and cafés in the Calle Paraná seemed to beckon to passersby with their warmth and friendliness. The yellowish light of the newspaper kiosk shone on famous faces in the magazines on display. The florist, a little farther on, was drinking *maté*. It was cold. Only in August is it ever as cold as that. I saw my brother walking slowly along, hands in his pockets. He went up to the newspaper vendor, shook hands with him, and they exchanged a few words. He continued on his way then he stopped and peered through the windows of Café 05—that was its name, El 05. He looked as though he really wanted to go inside.

The owner of the small tobacconist's stall called out to him as he went by. "Hey, Ariel, how are you?"

"Fine, and you?"

"You go on home, young man, it's getting really cold. They must be waiting for you."

"Yes, I'm going home now."

His voice was steady. He smiled and continued on his way.

I felt strange. He looked so lonely.

"Ariel!" I called after him. "Where have you been?"

"Hello, Gabriela. It's nice that we've run into each other."

I could see he was happy now. He wasn't alone anymore. "Shall we have a coffee before going home? Would you like to?"

Was it a feeling of happiness or belonging? I don't know what word I should use to describe that moment but I will always remember it.

We went into the café arm in arm as though we were a couple.

Years later, those same men— the newspaper vendor, the florist, and the tobacconist— stopped me in the street to express their condolences.

"Señorita, we miss your brother. He was a real gentleman. He knew how to take care of himself despite everything. We were very fond of him, Señorita, to tell you the truth, we miss him now."

The last time I saw my brother Ariel it was a winter day in Buenos Aires. He was sitting by the window, looking out onto the Plaza Vicente Lopez. He seemed calm. His hands lay crossed on the blanket over his knees. His gaze was lost at some point in the far distance.

I was in Paris when my sister Dora called me from Buenos Aires to tell me he was ill. He had already been unwell like that. I didn't want to lose any time so I took the next flight to Argentina.

I rode with him in the ambulance that brought him home from the hospital. I didn't leave the house for a week. I sat beside him and did some knitting while we talked. I helped him eat and read to him.

We recalled moments from our childhood, the stories and the mischievous things we'd gotten up to, each of us putting our own interpretation on them. Every morning, when our sister would leave to go to the office, we were left on our own with the maid, just like when we were children. In some way we had returned to our childhood where we had secrets we wouldn't share with anyone else.

The room had a large window. Ariel spent a great deal of time in bed or in Papá's chair, with a blanket over his knees. He felt the cold. He had difficulty walking. He got up in the morning, washed and dressed, and then put on Papá's paisley dressing gown. It was slightly too big for him but I think it made him feel protected as though Papá had his arms around him. It was an effort for him to shave. He put on aftershave and asked, "Do I smell nice?" He put on hair lotion and managed to keep looking his usual neat self. His face had become very thin. He tired very easily and would start trembling, unsteady. I would take his arm and say, "Straighten that back!"

Those were words our mother would say when we slouched.

He would sit in the worn, green velvet armchair in the corner of the bedroom. And I would bring in a tray with tea or *maté* and some biscuits and sit across from him. Elsewhere in the house all was quiet.

Ariel talked to me about the dreams he had had, of what he had never done and now never would. He told me about the girls he had liked but had never won. I tried to joke about each one of them, saying that one had been fat and that another had been unbelievably silly. He looked at me and agreed.

"I'll always be Mamá's little bear. I miss her. Do you miss her, Gabriela?"

I wanted to change the subject and talk about something else. But then he asked, "And Papá, don't you miss him?"

In the afternoons, he would lie down and rest. When he woke up I would help him walk as far as the sitting room. He wanted to sit by the window and look at the square below. He never asked to go out again. He was saying goodbye to everything, to each house and each tree.

He asked me to get a photograph album. We spent a lot of time like that. Sometimes we talked about the photos and sometimes we simply touched the faces of the people in them.

"We've changed so much, haven't we?"

In that album were photographs of Ariel at his first school. It was called Residencia Johnson. There were photos of him doing gymnastics with a teacher helping him so he could get a better sense of balance. In other photos he was with Juana and me, the three of us holding hands, dressed very formally, looking like well-behaved little children. He was wearing a tie, a white shirt, and gray flannel shorts. His shoes were so highly polished they still shine in that photograph. Juana and I were wearing taffeta and velvet dresses, and patent leather shoes. The school gardens were beautiful. It all seems like a dream now.

I cried and cried when I was on my own. I think he cried as well when he was alone. In our awkward way, we had gone back to being children.

They told me it wouldn't be long before he left us.

I went out for a walk. I would have liked him to be walking beside me.

I left him looking out of the window. I don't know if I even want to know what he was thinking.

He died one morning in October. It was early in the day. He simply collapsed and died while they were getting him dressed.

I was at a conference in Bucharest.

I can still picture him sitting in that chair by the window. I'm talking to him and we laugh and joke together.

In Almodóvar's movie *Volver*, the leitmotif is the tango of the same name. My brother and I thought we knew how to sing tangos. Our two best renditions were "Volver" and "Adios muchachos."

Back then I would never have thought that the words of those tangos would provide the key to the question I'm trying to answer now, as well as the question I faced all those years ago.

When I saw the movie it annoyed me. That was *my* song, *my* memories, and *my* unanswered question. I held on to it like a great secret and only brought it out very rarely. And when it was there, looking at me, facing me, I tried to ignore it. But it was very persistent. It wouldn't go back to the dark corner of my *kishkes*, as one says in Yiddish. It wouldn't go as far as my deepest feelings.

"Shut up, go to sleep and let me be."

"No. Tell me why you also won't go back, go back as the person you are now, the person you recognize, the person who knows you achieve the maximum. Accept yourself as you are."

"What do you want me to say? That I'm weak, that despite all the times I've gone back I still haven't found the answer?"

"You don't find it because you're not asking the right questions. I'm leaving now."

The memory left, but it kept coming back and knocking on the door to ask again.

* * *

At first, the Latin Americans at the university turned their backs on me because I was going out with an Englishman, the same man to whom I've been married for forty-eight years. But gradually, as they got to know him, they came to accept him.

When my parents first met him they inspected him closely, even with some degree of suspicion.

Only after thirty years of marriage did I begin to come into my own in asserting myself. I'm slow. I realize that now.

I couldn't open the door to the antechamber of my memories but something very different did. It was looking at me and telling me I should stop fooling myself. Notice I didn't say "lie." Cracks were beginning to form in the walls. The light was beginning to fight with the shadows and the wind with the stones of the past.

The past was very heavy and full of locks and bolts, a rusty can of worms.

Do you know, María, I can still remember the softness of your skin when I would kiss you before leaving the house. And also I can still remember your smell when you used to put me to bed, the way your clothes gave off a scent of cologne. I can remember the bottle. I've seen it here in the Paris pharmacies. It was Roger Gallet.

Má and Pá were often lying down, resting. I think it was always like that. It was the Saturday siesta. The household was asleep.

You waved goodbye to us and watched until we turned the corner and were out of sight. Once on the other side, Ariel and I would just look at each other and without saying anything we knew we were free.

With that freedom they gave us, they helped teach us respect. It helped us through our childhood and way beyond.

I was never afraid to open doors. I never felt that I wouldn't be able to deal with whatever I might come up against. I wonder if I've managed to instill the same feeling in my children.

"Ayala, be careful, don't go too near the edge, the snow might…"

I stop myself. I must not show that I don't have confidence in her ability to be careful on her own.

"Noemia, Mía, be careful…"

"Lara, be careful…"

So many times have I stopped myself when I remembered how my elders pressured me.

I look at my daughters and ask myself how it happened. They've already become three young women. But what about me? Where am I going?

We launch our children out into the world. Will they know how to survive in the desert? Will they, like birds, be able to find the water they need to keep them strong?

Will I ever be able to get off from this ever-moving ghost train without being scared?

* * *

We arrive at the tennis club. Howard has come with us.

I quickly go inside, looking for the young girl I used to be, and here I find the partitions and walls of my past.

"Mía, Lara, Ayala, come here! This was our changing room. Howard, you can't come in here."

While I show them around, I walk faster and faster; I want to get back all those lost hours.

"Mommy, it's just as you described it, the showers are all together," said Noemia.

The other two laugh, wandering around and looking at everything.

The changing room is almost empty. The sun is shining. There are people on the courts but as it's a weekday there isn't much activity.

They admire themselves in the mirror. Coquettish and mischievous. They know they're being looked at. We laugh without really knowing why. In just a few moments here, I think I've infected them with my happiness, that feeling of frivolousness the Czech writer Milan Kundera talks about.

We come out of the changing rooms to find Howard studying the old photographs displayed all over the walls.

"Everyone was so elegant. Look at the hats the women are wearing," says Lara.

They all come over to take a closer look. In those photographs they see another world. It's a small part of my parents' and my world and also the world they're beginning to discover for themselves.

"Let's have a drink outside."

The blue-and-white striped sunshades are gently flapping in the April breeze.

The sound of the racket hitting the ball and bouncing off the red courts sounds like music to my ears. There are some people talking as well. Everything takes on the balletic rhythm of each match.

"A lot has changed, and so have I," I tell my family.

"In what way have you changed, Mommy?" Ayala asks.

"Well, now I don't run to the tennis courts three times a week!"

They all laugh. No, I don't run and I don't play tennis anymore. I stopped doing any sports after my breast cancer operations. I'm not allowed to anymore.

"You see, Ayalita, tennis was my sport and no one else's in the family. I used to come here in the middle of the week and on weekends. I didn't get many invitations to go out with boys so my world revolved around sports. It was something where it didn't matter whether I had a boyfriend or not."

"Mommy, you're not ugly, what are you talking about?"

"Lara, no one invited me. I didn't know how to dance and I was very serious. Boys just got bored with me."

"So where did you learn how to dance so well?"

"I didn't learn, Noemia. I simply felt liberated as soon as I stepped onto the boat that took me to Israel."

Howard is smiling. "That's where she met Officer Nissim, who told her his life story and your mother was fascinated…"

"Would you like anything else to drink?" a waiter asks.

"You can tell they're tourists from the way they're dressed. Just listen to that accent. That'll help us, won't it, Pepe, but prices are rising."

"Well, Manuel, what do you expect? They come over here, loaded with dollars, and if they feel like it they just buy up half the country."

"Do you know what I heard? That the French keep on buying up companies and now they own half of Patagonia."

"Yes, I know. For them an apartment in the Barrio Norte sells at a rock bottom price."

"I've been told that in Paris, real estate sells at more than €5,000 per square meter. Do you realize how much that really is?"

"Waiter, would you bring us two Diet Coca-Colas, two fresh orange juices, and an infusion, please?"

"And what happened with the officer?" Ayala wants to know. Her black eyes are shining.

"Well, when I met him again in Haifa and he wasn't wearing his uniform anymore, it was all over. The uniform of an officer in the navy was a dream for us girls. It's not for nothing there's that old song, 'All the Nice Girls Love a Sailor.'"

"But how did Nissim take it? Wasn't he hurt?"

"No, Noemia, I think he was rather relieved that the slightly crazy, daydreaming young woman was going to leave him alone."

The girls all laugh and Howard joins in.

"Actually it wasn't that bad. He helped me get over José, the boyfriend who'd hurt me so much. He entertained me during the voyage."

What a world it was back then and how fickle I was. Perhaps I still am. I ponder this while looking at my little family.

"Mommy, why did you leave Argentina?" Noemia asks.

If I knew, if only I knew how to explain it all to them. "But I came back. I'm here with you now. I want to show you and tell you everything," I say very quietly.

"Mommy, you keep showing us schools, clubs, streets, and restaurants, but we want to know what the young Gabriela was like. Tell us something about her. Wasn't that the reason you came back here this time?"

Lara's eyes look stern. Her words are very direct but they don't hurt me. Why don't I feel hurt?

* * *

"Papá, do you have a minute, please?"

My father looked up from his papers, took off his glasses, and looked at me.

"Is something wrong? Don't you feel well?"

The walls of Papá's study were lined with books and files. There was one large window. His worn leather armchair, like the other chairs in the room, gave off a strong smell of the past.

"Papá, Marina has invited me to join her and two other girls and her aunt on a trip to Europe. Her aunt will be able to show us around and I…"

"That's out of the question. What's wrong with you, Gabriela? Why on earth do you want to travel like that and with people we don't know? Why, Gabriela?"

I didn't know how to answer him. I knew there was something inside me.

I looked at my father and understood that if I said what I was really feeling it would hurt him too much.

"Speak, Gabriela. I want an answer." My father's voice was shaking. Did he know? Could he sense it? Did he have a presentiment? Yes, I think so.

"Pá, I want to go away. I want to study somewhere else. I want to leave Buenos Aires. I feel I need to."

There was a long silence. My father was drinking his *maté*. I could sense what he was going to say.

"Travel, leave home, search for something new…" His tone of voice reflected a longing for other times. "I also left home. You know that. But the circumstances were very different. There were other reasons and other problems."

I didn't say anything but just let him talk. He would show me the way.

"Study? Certainly, you're right. But be honest with yourself, Gabriela, is that really all?"

I kept walking through them like scenes from a movie. The words, expressions, what my sisters had done and said; it's all there. I ran away from them, from a united, loving family that was going through the bad times of the Perón tyranny, the difficulties with my elder sisters' divorces, and there was my brother and his difficult circumstances. What right did I have to complain about anything? What was I complaining about anyway?

"Papá…"

"Freedom, Gabriela. Is that what you're looking for?"

I knew he would understand. We didn't talk about it anymore.

* * *

"Noemia, you're asking me why I made that journey, what I found and what I discovered? In turn, let me ask you, all three of you, what did you think you'd find out, what did you think you'd discover about me? Did you find anything? Tell me."

Ayala is looking at me very seriously but her eyes are gentle. My little girl who didn't talk until she was nearly four has the ability to convey her feelings discreetly but with such expression.

"Were you very unhappy when you were my age, Mommy?"

"I don't know if I would call it unhappiness exactly, but I felt so frustrated and I was really frightened."

* * *

The first few days I was in Jerusalem, I don't think I was homesick, really. Well, perhaps on Friday nights when I could see houses with their Shabbat candles lit and families together around the table.

As soon as I arrived I went to visit my father's brother and his wife. They lived in Tel Aviv. I took the bus from the central bus station in Jerusalem. I'm talking about the old station, not the one you use nowadays. It was small, stately, and filled with the happiness of bustling passengers carrying bags and packages bulging with presents and food. With time, I learned how to differentiate the various sections of the population according to which day they were traveling. On Sundays it was always soldiers and that hasn't changed even now. Thursday evenings and Friday mornings it was people going to visit their families in other cities. Israel is so small that one can travel from the north right down to the south in under four hours. Religious people and students go to Jerusalem. Apart from their being used to moving from place to place, they have relatives everywhere.

Nowadays things are different, not so much in the traditions but in the happy atmosphere that used to pervade the old central station. After being the target of so many terrorist attacks the station was rebuilt in another location. The new station is big and it's full of security personnel. We should be used to that by now but there's always tension. Smiles disappear when you see more security personnel than passengers. There was a time when none of us—I'm talking about my family and many others—dared travel by bus. You'd watch it on television, on the news programs, you'd see the images but they never told you how many people were killed or how many survived but now have to live the rest of their lives disfigured or mutilated. International news channels didn't tell you that.

On that first bus journey a young man who spoke Spanish sat down next to me. We began talking. I asked him things that made him laugh heartily several times. I can't remember his name but I can still picture his round face and large, smiling eyes. Also, I can remember he told me he was engaged. He told me how Jerusalem was like a large, very round bowl surrounded by hills and that one could walk right around the city just as though one were treading along the line of the circumference of a large circle. As we left the city, I saw the tanks of the War of Independence on the hills of Bab al-Wad. No one had moved them since the 1948 battles, in memory of the soldiers who had opened up the route to Jerusalem, which was then under siege with neither food nor water. Many died there. Among the commanders were Yitzhak Rabin, Yigal Allon, and many more who were to become the country's great leaders and heroes. The young man showed me the first palm trees as we got to Tel Aviv.

It wasn't difficult to find Motke and Zlote Goldemberg's house. I found myself standing in front of a small house with a smaller patch of land in front of it. The house looked poor. I knocked on the door and a smiling woman of medium height appeared. Her black hair was tied back in a bun and she wore an apron smudged with traces of cooking. As soon as she saw me she shouted, "Motke, it's Natán's daughter!"

My mouth dropped open in surprise. How on earth did she know who I was or whose daughter I could be?

Behind her there appeared a very straight-backed man with hair and beard as white as snow, wearing a *kippa*, a white shirt, and black pants. He was the very image of my father only many years older. He spoke Yiddish. I could understand what he was saying but didn't know enough to answer him. They sat me down on a bed. In the middle of the room there was a table and on the other side another bed. The beds also served as chairs.

Just inside the front door was the kitchen and through another door was the bathroom. My uncle looked at me and watched me. My aunt gave me a cup of tea and a slice of cake. I gave her the present I had brought, a large bottle of Christian Dior perfume. She took it, gave me a kiss, and thanked me. She looked at it, turning it over in her hands, and then put it away in her wardrobe.

Years later, when I opened that same wardrobe the bottle was still there.

My Uncle Motke was witness at my wedding. My Aunt Zlote, together with my sister-in-law Rachel, walked me to the chuppah.

We left the house where I had been living in Jerusalem. All the houses on that street were very old. Most of my neighbors were of Greek origin. The landlords of my building were from Thessaloniki. The husband was an electrician. He and his wife had been educated during the period of the British Mandate. Both of them kept the traditions from their former homes—coffee and *bourekas*, vine leaves stuffed with rice, and the festive songs with the ancient Sephardic intonation.

It was with his wife, Stella, that I went to the ritual bath before my wedding. Together we chose my veil, which I rented, in the religious district of Mea Shearim.

All the neighbors were standing in the doorways of their houses, waiting to bless the bride and congratulate her.

The synagogue was just a few steps away. I only had to cross the street.

My husband-to-be was already there. He had been signing the marriage contract papers, as tradition demanded.

It was then I realized that in some way my decision to get married alone, without my parents present, was of some significance. My uncle and aunt represented all the other family members who weren't there.

Only once did I sleep on one of those divan beds in my uncle and aunt's house. It was a magical night. I slept so peacefully. The feather pillows, fresh sheets, the quiet and the warmth wrapped around me and carried me far away. When I woke up, my aunt's smiling face was there to welcome me into the very private world they had built together. She brought me a cup of tea.

"We have to spoil you, you're alone in Jerusalem. You're studying and I'm sure you're not eating properly or sleeping enough."

I just didn't know what to say. I smiled at her, drank my tea, and ate the cake she always baked on Fridays.

After that, they always sent me to one of their son's houses. They said I'd be more comfortable there.

Sometime later, I asked my cousins about that branch of the family that had lived through the war. I wanted to understand how they had managed to survive. My father never told us that story, about those who stayed behind in Europe.

My cousins showed me photographs. There was one of my uncle in his Austro-Hungarian uniform, another of my aunt, looking radiant, and others showing my cousins, when they were with the partisans, and my uncles who had been taken away to the concentration camp in Romania and later to the British prison camp in Cyprus.

They preferred to talk of the past avoiding any mention of those years. But I persisted in asking them to tell me all about it.

* * *

We get out of the car on the boulevard that led to the pharmacy Uncle Saul used to have in the neighboring town of San Antonio de Padua. Uncle Saul, my mother's brother, had studied pharmacy and married a woman who was so beautiful she looked like a movie star. They had two sons. My uncle played tennis and had a wonderful voice. They used to say my sister Dora had inherited her voice from my mother's side of the family and so she took singing lessons. Her voice didn't seem like anything special to me.

I want my daughters to see our former country house in Merlo, some fifteen minutes away, but I don't recognize the road. Something's missing but I don't know what. My forehead is burning and my mouth is so dry I feel that I simply must get out of this place. These eyes of mine, searching for the past, aren't the same as those that witnessed things, events, landscapes, and people's faces all those years ago. Perhaps I imagined it all and what's in my mind is just a fairytale, like when I was very small and played under the fruit trees.

We go into the town hall. The staff searches in the relevant ledgers for some information on the country house "Villa Perlita" and find nothing. Absolutely nothing. The land had been divided up and everything had been altered, even in the land registers. It had all disappeared. I am so upset I want to shout and cry. It seems like a sin. It had all been erased. But the place my memory has awakened is still more tangible than the memory itself. For some time now I have thought that a way of understanding a city and its inhabitants is to puzzle out, to work out the attitude, or rather, how people deal with and how they understand the architecture, the structure, lines, and stones of their old buildings and districts. But how do *I* see them, these ruins of a geography I left behind when I was a girl, whole buildings that seem to have been allowed to blow away with the winds from the pampas?

I go over to the window with its colonial railings like bars of memory that are still there but prevent me from going to meet my childhood. I'm like a prisoner.

I need to remember so that I can know where I'm going and with whom. Not everything I see is always clear. It seems to be permanently linked to innumerable, almost identical scenes but the lenses are out of focus, accentuating the kaleidoscopic effect. Sometimes the scene is scratched when it's a tragic one, as with any work considered a saga.

The boulevard across from the church is still there. When I was small and I saw that church, I knew it meant we were getting close to our country house. We would turn to the left and onto a wide road between rows of very slender trees. We would also pass in front of a slaughterhouse. I remember how the mere mention of that word scared me.

I go out onto the balcony to look at the colonial courtyard. I can see men in gray suits carrying papers and files, going from one office to another. There's something gloomy about them in their grayness and their worn-out shoes. There's no happiness there. The plants seem to say, "Look at us, we're still flourishing despite everything." The many people going up and down the stone staircase have worn away the steps and even the clicking keys of the typewriters can't shake off the dusty atmosphere.

"Then where is the neighboring Hussay estate?" I ask the poor employee who seems totally lost in the midst of all my questions despite wanting to do his job and demonstrate his competence. Bothered by his inability to help me, he starts giving orders to his secretary to show that at least he still has some power left. The situation becomes almost farcical with the woman trying to understand what he's saying to her but not daring to ask him for any further explanation. She turns around and leaves the office, closing the door very quietly behind her. Shortly afterward, she gently opens it again and says apologetically, "Señora, I'm so sorry but I'm afraid I can't find that file."

"But how's that possible? Señorita, keep looking for it…what will the Señora think? That we don't have our papers in order here?" The official mutters but his voice still conveys authority.

The woman is wearing a black skirt and white blouse. Her dry hair is white at the roots. She should have had it dyed a while ago. Her hands are dry as well and her eyes look dull. Some of her teeth are missing and her shoes are very worn. She doesn't answer him but just lowers her head as though the weight of the world is on her shoulders.

Is this today's Argentina that I've been dreaming about? Is this the country that claims to be part of the first world? With its poverty and wretchedness so apparent?

"Yes, Señor. I'll keep looking."

"Señora, we can't find those registers. I don't know what could have happened. Please understand, we would like to help you."

"Yes, I know, I'm sure you're trying to help me but you must understand that I feel…almost as though part of my life and my family's life has simply been erased."

"Señora…if you wish to, you could send a letter to the municipality of…"

"Look, Señor," the secretary says, interrupting him. "Here are the title deeds of the area but I can't find…"

"May I have a look, please?"

I take the file. The yellowing sheets of paper seem to disintegrate as I touch them.

I realize it's a waste of time. I don't know the names of the lawyers, the notaries, the solicitors, and administrative councils—it all appears to be very organized but it's a system with which I'm not at all familiar.

I turn around to look at my daughters who are looking worriedly at me. How can I possibly convey it all to them—the smells, the fears, the tears, and the dreams of the person I was in that house?

Who was I back then? I asked myself.

I appeal to the girls, "I need to talk to you. I want to explain the reason for this journey of ours. I want to hear your comments and see what you're thinking. Don't leave me in this empty space. Help me find myself again by telling me what you see and what you think. I'm asking you to hold my hand."

There, I said it. I've bared myself. Now the ball is in my daughters' court.

* * *

"Let's leave now," Má said. "Papá is waiting for us in the car."

It was a black car and remembering it now, I think it was squarish. We all climbed in and there was room for everyone. Well, Ariel wasn't with us. He was away at boarding school. It was called the Residencia Johnson, an English school. He lived there. Some weeks we saw him on Sundays and other weeks only Pá and Má went to visit him. Sometimes they went to see him during the week as well. When they came home they were sad and quiet. That private, silent world belonged to them both. Sometimes I heard my grandmother asking my mother how the boy was. "How's Lebele?" she asked. That's what she called him. In Yiddish that word means "life" in its affectionate, shortened form. I know they were talking about my brother Ariel.

One bright, cold, winter Sunday we left early for the *quinta* estate. We were going to see the country house for the first time. My parents were so happy they'd bought it, especially Papá. He liked being in the country, he loved the land. His father, his grandfather, his great-grandfather, and many earlier generations of his family grew wheat and tobacco in Russia. They told me that people called my grandfather the lord of wheat. I was very small. I could hardly be more than four years old but I knew I felt much bigger and I certainly felt very important.

The morning was cold and there was mist. I knew there was mist. The air was white but with shadows dancing to the rhythm of the music of the wind in the cypresses. It was a big, square house with a courtyard at its center off which so many doors opened! The floors had dark red tiles that shone like blood. The kitchen was enormous like all the other rooms and had large flagstones on the floor, windows all around, and a high ceiling. Firewood heated the stove for cooking and in the middle of the kitchen was a large table. A door led through to another room that was cold and rather dark even after they put in a window. That was where all the provisions were kept. The "pantry" they called it.

The swimming pool was on top of a hill covered with the greenest grass. All around there were colorful flowers. In front of the pool there was a windmill that stood like a watchtower making sure everything was in order in our little world. Perhaps that's why we had to climb some white steps to go inside. Farther on was the garage with the *break* and the *sulky* carriages near the work tools and stacks of fodder for the animals. It seemed that no one ever opened those stacks of fodder. When the grown-ups were having their siesta us children would hide there, especially if the weather was cold. I would follow Juana around.

During holidays Ariel would come too. We used to love going across the fields in those horse-drawn carts. As far as I was concerned that was absolute proof that the stories and tales I read about didn't only belong to a fantasy world. There were fields, fruit trees, horses, cows, flowers, gardens designed like English gardens, and manicured lawns as soft as green velvet. There were so many birds. Some were strange and frightening. A pair of peacocks would strut about the garden, and there was a flamingo so pink it looked as though it had been painted, and white storks with black beaks. That was where I first saw a stork, the bird that María said had the marvelous mission of producing babies. As soon as I saw it I unquestioningly, enthusiastically embraced this world of animals and carriages. I decided it would be the backdrop to my dreams. And to that I added the stories by Alexandre Dumas that I couldn't stop reading. Later on, I read the novels of Charles Dickens, the

Comtesse de Ségur, Louisa May Alcott, Jane Austen, the Brontë sisters, and other books that my mother decided would provide me with a solid grounding in literature. She was convinced that if one knew nothing of English or Russian literature, the works of Gorki or the German writer Hubermann, then one couldn't possibly have any understanding of *Kultur*.

A couple of caretakers lived in a house nearby. Their job was to look after the house when we weren't there and make sure everything was ready for us when we arrived. María was always with us and so was Don Segura, Papá's trusted friend.

I didn't like the hens or the birds shut up in cages. One summer, Mamá let them out. I don't know why, perhaps because none of us liked seeing them imprisoned like that.

That was where I tasted my first blackberry, where I went to sleep under the peach trees, and where I bathed my dolls at the foot of the windmill. It was there they gave me my pony. I found a name for him right away—*Petiso* (Little One). Papá had brought him all the way from Buenos Aires. When they arrived, at first the pony simply refused to come out of the horse box, and then all of a sudden something must have changed his mind and out he jumped neighing loudly. We all laughed. That was how we welcomed him.

Mamá used to spoil me a lot. She bought me my first riding outfit, all in red. The bulls used to chase me across the fields. My father said I should be firm and show the pony who was master. I think that was the only reason I didn't fall off. Much, much later I taught my own daughters to ride when they were still very young, passing on to them what my father had taught me. I told them it would build character.

Lara must have been only about eight when a horse refused a jump and she went flying over its head.

I was sitting in the stands around the manège where the children were having their riding lessons. Instinctively I stood up to go to her, but the look the instructor shot at me made me sit down again, without a word of protest.

"Rider, get back on that horse immediately!"

Lara picked up her helmet and, looking very serious, she coolly got back on the horse.

I remember what my father said. It seems that falling off like that and self-control helped him face many difficult situations later in life when self-assurance served him in good stead, what I have heard described as "facing off."

In my case, I simply don't know if I've really been self-assured or if I just give the impression of being so, or whether in fact it is because I learned how to internalize old resentments and questions I was never brave enough to formulate. But there are also other things, things I now wish I hadn't left unsaid, particularly when I was at school and I didn't say what I was thinking to my girlfriends for fear of losing their friendship.

For as long as I can remember I've felt different from everyone else. I often thought about being different but never talked to anyone about it. I did what was expected of me and behaved as I was supposed to. I didn't really think about what I wanted in life nor did I even know what that was until much later on. But when I did eventually realize what I really wanted, it was like unleashing an avalanche of resistance and uncontrollable thoughts that began to smother me.

My sisters used to think I was conceited because of the way I behaved. My longing for independence meant I was often in my room with the door closed so that I could be alone with my books and my thoughts. My mother asked me to control the "ugly beast," which was how she referred to my spells of shutting myself off from the rest of the family. My father said I must be a "pillar of stone" because of my lack of reaction to things. I kept all my emotions bottled up inside.

My parents saw me from their own individual viewpoint: my mother's view of me was colored by her confrontations with my father, my father's through his own need for space. They did not understand that it was all reflected in my silence. He used to shut himself up in his study with the paper and some *maté*. He was always dressed the same: dark gray pants, white shirt, dark tie, and white cardigan. My mother didn't like him to wear colored shirts. Just once, when they came back from Europe, Papá wore some needlecord shirts. He had bought a couple while he was there, one navy and one dark brown.

I've come back here with my daughters to try and find that young girl and say to her, "Look what I have become. Do you recognize me? Do the streets of Buenos Aires recognize me, the fields in the country, the dryness of the north and the hospital where I was born? Is this what destiny held in store for me or did I destroy my dreams?" It's as though the young girl is talking to me and I'm listening to her.

I've tried to tell you, to get you to feel what all this meant for the young girl I was back then—the fields and those years when we were there, what my childhood and later my adolescence were actually like. What it meant to grow up amidst these smells and colors, the rain, the secrets and tears. But it has all vanished.

It was a golden time for the family. My parents were young, they went to parties and won prizes dancing the *raspa*. I loved my mother's mink stole. I'd wrap it around my shoulders and walk about, trailing it behind me. María would say I was mopping the floor with it whenever she caught me. I used to love opening my mother's perfume bottles and pots of cream with their intoxicating smells that seemed so exotic to me. Sitting on their big double bed I would play with my mother's jewelry, touching and looking at it all with wonder. There I found yet more proof that the fairytale princesses I read about really did exist.

There was a time—I must have been about four or five—when something threatened the enchanted life we were leading. I can remember my parents talking together in hushed tones and my sisters' stony silence. As I was very young I suppose I must have been totally excluded from what was going on. It's only my memory of it now that lets me understand. There were no more holidays or horses, we didn't go to the country house anymore, and Papá's hair became grayer and grayer. All of these facts pointed to the family's dire financial situation.

A colonel called Juan Domingo Perón had come to power. His wife, Evita, was very pretty with fair hair and a broad smile. She talked a lot. They said they were helping and that they loved the people of Argentina. They promised there would be no more poverty. It was a long time before I understood the full implication of it all. Our meals were often in silence and there were many sad times. Jewelry and property were sold, and my father's face became lined and his hair went white. There was sadness in the house with my mother grumbling and my sisters staying quietly in their bedrooms. And there were new words I kept hearing like expropriation, bribery, and corruption.

They said there was a revolution. The pervading feeling was one of fear and yet everything seemed to be the same.

Then a change came about.

* * *

Noemia's voice brings me back to reality: "Mommy, we're going back to the city."

She's looking at me with understanding in her eyes. In her firm, decisive way, Lara calls the driver and goes back to the car, followed by Ayala. The little one follows her elder sisters.

I say goodbye to the employees who are standing with us. I can sense their discomfort.

"Thank you, you've helped me…"

"No, Señora, we can see you're upset. We do apologize but, well, you know, there were so many changes and sometimes places were even burned, you do understand?"

"Yes, I understand. It's not easy to protect the past. Thank you and good afternoon."

"Good luck, Señora, good luck."

As I walk away, back to the car, I turn around to look at them one more time. I can't help waving to them and wishing them good luck as well.

The air all around them is full of the smell of barbecued meat. It's lunch time. Just for a moment I feel like stopping the car and going to eat in one of those restaurants. Perhaps it would help me tell my daughters what the barbecues were like at the *quinta*. How we used to put the branches on at four in the morning to get the fire going. Then we would add the offal and then whatever animal it was, lamb usually, and plenty of it, for all the people who would be eating with us that day. My father would drink his *maté,* and he'd always be wearing his beret set to one side and his old leather jacket. He would chat with Don Segura, trying to predict whether there'd be rain or fine weather.

I think Don Segura came from Santiago del Estero. He was dark with a flat nose and eyes that shone like coals. He was the son of a white woman and a man with some trace of African blood in his veins. He used to walk with his back slightly bent. He didn't like to address us children but preferred to talk to Papá, whom he called El Patrón. Later on, he would talk to my brother when he was back from boarding school. El Patroncito, The Little Boss, he called him. They all knew and understood my parents' sorrow. They knew Ariel would never be the boss. His innocent face told them that, his features those of a boy with Down's syndrome.

When I was at school and chatting with my girlfriends, I never spoke of my brother, I didn't listen to their questions, or their words and expressions of commiseration. He never came to pick me up from school or to any play we were putting on, nor did he take part in any national festivities. In fact my parents hardly ever came either. I think that throughout my school years—I mean both primary and secondary—my parents were only able to come twice or at most three times. I was sorry they didn't come to see me perform or whatever it was we were doing at school, but I don't think it really bothered me that much. It seemed normal to me, just as they didn't know much about my life or my problems inside those cold, austere classrooms. I was never a very good student, although I don't know why. I think it didn't interest me very much. As I got older I would just get home from school, do my homework, and then burrow into whatever book I was reading. On the weekend we would go to the sailing club where I would spend all my time playing tennis or ping-pong, and then there'd be a snack toward the end of the day.

My brother was always impeccably dressed. Both at school and at home he'd put a lot of effort into washing and being dressed correctly with a good haircut, polished shoes, and his fingernails nicely trimmed. Yes, that's what I most remember about him—his warm, soft, small hands.

One winter's day, I thought that helping with the gardening might show the grown-ups how good we were being. So after lunch, when the house was all quiet, I told my brother about my idea and we went out to the garden.

"Arielito," I said, "let's put the tallest ladder against the walnut tree, then we can reach up and pick all the nuts and take off their green outer shells. What do you think, is that a good idea?"

Ariel, of course, was more than happy to agree to such an escapade. We climbed up the ladder together, one on either side, and began our work. We pulled at the branches to get hold of the walnuts and then picked them.

"Gabriela, look at the color of our hands, they've turned all green!" Ariel said, frightened.

"Oh, don't worry about that. It's nothing. It'll all come off with soap and water." There were still plenty of walnuts on the branches so I kept on picking. And then all of a sudden the ladder began to sway and rock from side to side. We were stuck halfway up.

That's when I panicked.

"What should we do now?" I ask Ariel. He wasn't crying nor was I but I was frightened, not of falling off but of what they were going to say to us.

We called out for María but there's no way she could have heard us where we were. Would anyone be able to hear us calling for help?

Then Don Segura arrived on the scene. He looked very serious and with his big, strong hands he lifted us down off the ladder and set us back on the ground. He didn't say a word and his face had a blank expression just like the Indians in the films we'd seen about the Far West.

"Go back to the house." That was all he said.

Our parents scolded us but they also laughed at our antics.

"We only wanted to help," we said.

"Help? You're lucky you didn't both break your legs. Now get into the bath right away and we'll say nothing more about it."

Ariel and I looked at each other. We knew what the other was thinking—that we'd never forget our little adventure for as long as we lived!

Our hands and fingernails were stained green for a long time despite all the soap and scrubbing.

I miss him. He died very quietly. He simply left us one day. I also remember another hand, smaller and very cold.

July 1974

It was a gray winter's day when the air seemed full of fear and secrecy.

We were living in Mexico. Howard was working at the university and I was with the Israeli embassy. We traveled to Argentina with our two daughters. I felt I needed to visit Buenos Aires with them before the end of our stint in Mexico and our return to Israel.

We were excitedly looking forward to our visit. I hadn't seen my mother since my father had died. My sister, Adela, invited us to stay with her. I've never understood why I accepted. It was a complete and utter nightmare.

Under a leaden sky the streets of Buenos Aires reflected poverty. Everything was quiet. While we walked around we began to understand the true meaning of the word "sinister." The hunger for freedom was written all over people's faces but fear prevented them from saying anything. Ghosts began to confuse me, pushing me toward the house that had been my home but had rejected me.

It had been such a long time since I'd walked along these fondly remembered streets. No one could have known whether they were drops of rain or tears of desperation for the people that made me so cold and feel so much bitterness.

My mother didn't see me but I saw her. She was watering the plants on the balcony. Dusk was falling and on the other side of the square I was praying she would see me standing there, hoping by some miracle she would recognize me.

She hadn't replied to any of my letters and had refused to see my friends who tried to bring her news about me and my little family. My pride, my stupid pride stopped me from going up to the door, ringing the bell, and hugging her.

She had been told that I was demanding my share of the inheritance and that I had been speaking against the family. Many more years were to go by before we spoke to each other.

* * *

In July 1976, the fourth of July to be precise, an Air France plane bound for Paris was hijacked shortly after taking off from Tel Aviv. It landed in Uganda. That was what led to the now famous Operation Entebbe.

I was in Buenos Aires at the time, listening to contradictory reports, some of which were violently anti-Semitic and anti-Israeli. It all happened very quickly.

Howard had already left. I was traveling back to Mexico with my little daughters. Lara was five then and Noemia was only three and a half. At Ezeiza Airport I bought them some chocolate, knowing they would probably ask for something sweet on the flight. The weather in Buenos Aires was still gray and rainy.

The flight took off as scheduled. We hadn't eaten since breakfast. There hadn't been time and the children were getting hungry. I felt free and all I wanted was to get back to our home in Mexico, have a bath, and sit in the kitchen with some coffee. And, of course, to get back to Howard.

No more than ten minutes into the flight they announced we would be landing in Montevideo. They gave no explanation. The plane landed and all the passengers were taken to one side in a separate part of the airport. My children could see the enticing duty free shops with their displays of colorful sweets and drinks but we were not allowed to buy any.

There was a meningitis epidemic in Uruguay at that time. I accosted every airline employee I could see and asked why we had landed in Montevideo. Either they didn't know or they didn't answer me. It seemed they didn't even understand Spanish. We were taken back to the plane without having eaten or drunk anything. We were told that because of the epidemic, the airline didn't want to risk serving contaminated food on board.

I gave my children some of the chocolate. I don't know why but I rationed it and only gave them a small piece each.

Then they informed us we were now bound for Peru where the plane would take food on board. We all went to sleep.

The plane didn't land in Peru. Flight control refused to clear us for landing as we'd come from an airport with health issues. The flight continued north—or so they told us. Then the announcement came that we would be landing in Colombia.

There was unusual silence in the cabin, very unusual considering the number of passengers on board. The only voices to be heard were those of the flight attendants whispering to one another. I tucked in the children as best I could, hoping it would help them go to sleep. I didn't want them to sense my anxiety. The lights over the seats came on instructing us to fasten our seatbelts.

"You'll see, we'll be eating something wonderful in a little while." I don't know if that was what they wanted to hear me say but the children just looked at me and smiled.

The passengers did as they were told and obediently walked off the plane, like lambs to the slaughter.

There were soldiers everywhere with army trucks parked alongside the runway. There were no explanations, nothing. All was quiet.

The room they took us to had blindingly bright lights. There were benches along the walls. We sat there and waited. A large box served as a platform for a short soldier who strutted into the room and went over to stand on it. He yelled at us:

"Right, all of you, outside on the runway. Open your baggage, we need to do an inspection!"

We hurried out of the room. The uniforms were intimidating. There we were, on the vast runway, in the middle of the night, each of us opening up our suitcases and undoing our bags.

The wind began to scatter the lighter items. With the butt of their machine guns the soldiers poked and turned over the contents of everyone's luggage. There were so many armed soldiers all around us, we didn't protest but just let them get on with it.

We got back on the plane again. We didn't even dare ask for a glass of water. At that point, the plane's cabin seemed the safest place for us.

The children were beginning to look pale and tired and I could see their lips were becoming dry. I closed my eyes and tried not to notice anything else. I looked for our passports in my bag. Something told me to hide my Israeli passport.

"Señora, listen to me, please."

The flight attendant touched my shoulder and bent down to say something. She almost whispered in my ear, "We're going to land again, don't ask me anything. I'm just telling you because you're the only passenger with small children. When we land, get off the plane as fast as you can and run. Run!"

Once again, the captain's voice came over the speaker: "We're landing again. Fasten your seatbelts."

I looked at my bag.

"Lari, Mía, we have to get off the plane again."

They looked at me without saying anything. We left the plane and I ran, carrying Noemia in one arm and holding tightly onto Lara's hand with the other.

All the passengers were running.

We found we'd been taken back to the same place, the same white room. It looked like an interrogation room.

I was right. The short soldier was there. Angrier than ever, yelling, his face red and moist with sweat.

"Who's the terrorist? Who placed those bombs?"

There was deathly silence. We were petrified. They divided us into groups: men, women, children, Americans and Latin Americans. With my children they took me over to another group.

"What's this?" the police officer asked, taking my eyeliner out of my bag.

"Makeup."

"Take her away."

I turned round and asked one of the nuns traveling with us, "Please look after my children."

They gave me a piece of paper and my eyeliner.

"Write!" barked the sergeant.

"What do you want me to write?" I asked him in such a calm voice it surprised even me.

"What you wrote on the plane, woman!"

"I don't know what you're talking about."

"On the mirror in the toilets, damn you, what you wrote about the bombs!"

"But I'll write whatever you want me to, just tell me what…"

They didn't let go.

I wrote something. I can't remember what. Whatever came into my head. They took the piece of paper and looked over toward my children, smiling at them. The children were watching me, very serious expressions on their little faces. The nun was standing beside them.

After what seemed an eternity, during which I kept looking over at my briefcase to see if it was still closed, they returned my eyeliner to me and ordered me to go back and sit with the others.

I hugged my children. All I could think of was giving them something to eat and drink; the poor little things hadn't had anything for hours. I knew I had to keep calm.

"Mommy, I need to go to the bathroom," Noemia said. I got up to take them both.

"Where do you think you're going?" A soldier rudely barred the way. "No one's leaving here."

"But it's the children, they need to go to the bathroom."

He pushed me with the butt of his gun. It was painful. Little Noemia couldn't hold it in any longer. She watched in dismay as a puddle formed around her feet.

Six o'clock in the morning and the journalists began to arrive. We could see them through the glass partitions.

"You're to talk to no one, and you're to make no signs to anyone," shouted one of the soldiers.

The short soldier came in. He looked haggard. We were all so exhausted and hungry that the scene became almost dreamlike. He stepped up on the box again to give himself more height and importance.

"The plane is ready. Prepare to go."

More and more passengers began to ask questions. But once again, there were no answers given. They didn't know.

"Did they find the bombs?" No answer.

They brought us milk, juice, and water.

"What's happening? Are we getting back on the plane or staying here?"

Some men in business suits who looked like executives of some sort asked permission to go and buy some wine.

"Look, whether we're leaving now or if we're going to get blown up we might as well have some good wine."

I got back on board with the children. The nuns followed behind us, praying their rosary beads.

Before we landed in Mexico I asked the children not to say anything to Howard about the bombs.

During the flight some of the passengers were exorcising their fear by singing: "*Para bailar la bomba, para bailar la bomba, se necesita un poquito de gracia…y una chispita….*" It seemed they must have found some wine after all.

Howard was waiting for us at the foot of the gangway. The children ran into his arms shouting, "*La bomba, Papá, para bailar la bomba!*"

We later learned they had found two bombs. There had been terrorists on that flight.

The following Monday I went to the doctor. I had lost the baby. I had been three months pregnant.

* * *

I look at my girls. They smile at me.

"Shall we go and eat, Mommy?"

"Well, my tummy's certainly rumbling already," Ayala says.

"Yes, my loves. It's just that sometimes I let myself get carried away by memories with their dramas and then it's so wonderful to get back to you!"

"Let's look for somewhere that's outside," suggests Noemia.

"All right. Why don't we try this place?"

We pay the taxi driver and get out. We are in one of the Bajo streets, across from an old church where the inner courtyard has been converted into a restaurant. Most of the houses around the church date from the early 1900s. They could do with a good coat of paint and the streets and pavements are in urgent need of repair. But even so, the small, narrow streets like Balcarce and San Martín have managed to retain their charm.

The people living here are the guardians of the past, entrusted with looking after and fiercely protecting the district from invasions of enormous skyscrapers like those that were built during Señor Menem's neoliberal development epidemic. And over there, standing proudly, is the Torre de los Ingleses, but its clock doesn't work anymore. Beyond the Retiro station, the Plaza San Martín tries hard to retain its air of dignity despite all the ugly stalls and kiosks that have sprung up.

"Come, let's have something to eat in this one." It's me talking. My voice sounds calm and controlled, clear of any emotion. "What do you think? It's not every day one gets to eat in what was once a colonial convent."

In the Buenos Aires of 2003 it's very fashionable to open restaurants in unusual places. Argentine society has been through it all: dictatorship under the generals, the supposed democracy of Alfonsín, who offered dreams of an elected government by and for the people but that was, in fact, led by a cultural élite—but once again the people were deceived and that was all they were left with, deception. There have been other governments, there have been the demonstrations of the Madres de la Plaza de Mayo and the protesters banging on pots and pans. But somehow the country always manages to keep moving ahead. Argentinians are very good workers—that's how they see themselves and believe it to be true. They have great difficulty taking any criticism and they have equal difficulty in considering themselves Latin Americans. I'm so glad I left the country but at times it can be painful. And I'm not even thinking of this morning's fruitless search.

Between here and there, between now and then, the many fragments of the puzzle are pieced together, touching on past, present, and future. I must not avoid situations but rather embrace the blessing of being here, now, in the present. A moment of grace where everything has meaning.

The thick convent walls block out the sound of traffic and the polluted air. The way to the bathroom is along wide, chilly cloisters. At the far end of a hallway are heavy wooden doors barring access to the cells. Perhaps there are ghosts walking around beyond those doors.

The old quarter of Buenos Aires, over there by the Avenida de Mayo, has a charm all its own. The tunes of the old tangos, with the accordion crying on each note, float along the narrow streets in such a way that one begins to walk in time to the music. It opens up the shutters on old memories. If you keep watching and concentrate, you'll see couples dancing just like those depicted on souvenir postcards. What has changed since the days of handsome Rudolf Valentino? Everything is almost exactly the same. A woman is carrying a tray piled high with the thinnest of *tacos*, her lips painted with blood-red lipstick, her dress hugging her figure, and her long black hair done up in a large coil on top of her head. The man walking beside her has oiled his hair and he wears his hat at a rakish angle that almost covers one eye. In the pocket of his white-striped, dark suit, there's a silk handkerchief that seems about to fall as it moves with each step he takes. From his insolent, bold gaze to his pointed, patent leather shoes, he presents a living image of the past.

The dramatic element is in the cry of the accordion's notes. Death looms, maybe grappling with the blade of the knife wielded by a despairing lover. The cigarette will fall from the lips of the one who is wounded, abandoned, but the dying gaze follows the couple. The audience waits anxiously, frightened, for the dénouement of the tragedy. It is both theater and reality.

Ya estoy viendo que esta noche vienen del sur los recuerdos,[2] around me and inside me I can hear the words of that Borges *milonga*.

Noemia is smiling, watching her mother. She seems to be in a reverie, so absorbed in her memories. "Mommy, you're thinking about dancing, aren't you."

Those words break down the thin wall that had been separating me from my daughters and bring me back to reality and the present. The notes of the past will still be there, floating in the white air, in the March heat.

---

2 Tonight I am watching the memories come up from the south.

Later on we will travel to the south, the north, to Salta and Jujuy. The suitcases are already packed.

* * *

"Hacoach" is the name written over the entrance to the club that played such an important part in my young life. Here I am, standing in front of the iron gates, and I'm simply astounded at the number of security staff there are both inside the gates and out here on the sidewalk. When I was a child there was a sort of hut at the entrance with a man inside. I can't remember if he wore any uniform or not. But nowadays that's the extent to which the Jewish community here needs to protect itself. They talk about anti-Semitism, attacks, and, of course, no one forgets the bombs at the AMIA and in the Israeli embassy. But seeing security like that at my tennis club, in the gardens where I played as a child, sends shivers down my spine.

It has changed a great deal. It's enormous now, with far more tennis and basketball courts than there used to be. And there are even grills for having barbecues. My family follows me around. I'm walking faster and faster. I'm looking for something. Yes, of course, there's the old house you could sleep in if you wanted to spend the night there. But…but what's this?

"Howard," I call to my husband, "look, it isn't here, it isn't here anymore…"

"What isn't here anymore? What's the matter?"

"The building where we used to get changed, the showers, everything that used to be above the bar…"

It was there, in those showers, that I discovered I'd started my first period. I felt cheated. I know it's silly, only a detail, but that's where I became a woman.

From the sloping jetty we can see the river. I think I'm hearing my sister Adela's voice calling me to go rowing with her.

No, it is my mind playing tricks again. It is Ayala calling me. "Mommy, I want to try doing some rowing. Can we?"

"No, not today. You're not dressed for it."

But she's already sitting in the dinghy and taking hold of the oars. "Mommy, look at me, I can do it!"

Howard takes a photo of her. She's smiling and looks so happy.

And here I am, facing voices of the past and shadows of the present.

My mother reclining in the same deckchair, under the trees. I could see her chatting with Señora Parnes. My father was sitting a little farther on, playing dominos with Señor Parnes and smoking a cigarette.

Ariel was waiting for me to play ping-pong with him. He used to love that game. He didn't come here much but when he did, we spent all the time playing together. He was my partner in everything. We used to have such fun, laughing together. And every now and then we'd go to find Papá to ask for some money to buy milk and sandwiches.

We wouldn't get back to the city until the evening when night was falling. Sometimes I'd fall asleep in the car on the way home. I hated the very thought that the next day was Monday, which meant school. During the summer we'd pull in to eat at a restaurant called The Munich. There, we'd have German sausage and sauerkraut, beer for Papá and Mamá, and orange juice for us.

When the factory closed and the money problems became even more acute, the first thing to be sold was the estate. I didn't know about that until I found the name plaques from the house—Villa

Perlita—that Papá had put away in his desk. Those plaques from the entrance to the *quinta* had been like signs of welcome to the house

Papá was quiet. Very quiet. I offered to bring him some *maté*, knowing that if I did it, it would be like passing a test. To prepare it properly, the water must not be boiling, there should be just the right amount of *yerba*, not too much and not too little, the small spoonful of sugar must not be too full and none of it could spill before getting to the study.

There was an image of my father that will always be with me: he was sitting behind his enormous desk, so big it could have served as a dining table. There was a lamp on the desk and papers everywhere. He had mysterious boxes that all closed when a single key was inserted only in the lock of the middle box. His chair was a swivel chair. Ariel and I, when we were very young, would spin each other around in it. One day we made it spin around too fast and Ariel fell off the chair onto something sharp and metal. He cut his tongue. I'll never forget how furious my father was. Nor will I ever forget the sound of his voice as sharp as that piece of metal.

My father picked my brother up in his arms and carrying him ran out to the car. I didn't know whether to cry or run outside with them. I started to laugh. It must have been a nervous reaction. Ariel had to have some stitches in his tongue. It altered his speech for a while. To frighten me, he would stick out his tongue and show me the stitches. It made us laugh.

* * *

We went back to Merlo. There was a barbecue under the trees. We all sat down around the table where we'd had so many meals before. Over on the other side was our house but now it was full of people I didn't know. I didn't want to look and I didn't want them to see me. We never went back again after that barbecue. I don't know what became of our *sulkys* and horses and all the other animals.

All that we had left of the house were those plaques with the name on them. And now I don't even know what became of them either.

* * *

I appreciate my daughters' silence.

I'll look for photos of those years, photos of the family and the house and my horse. I'll find them in my sister Dora's bookcase.

"Look, here's my mother and here's my father on his horse, Rubia. He wouldn't let anyone else ride her."

"And who's the little girl posing in the pretty dress?" asks Noemia, who already knows the answer.

"That's me! It's true, I was pretty, wasn't I."

"The image of Noemia. You look exactly the same," Lara says.

"Now we know where she gets her coquetry from!"

My sister is listening to us. She's looking at us but doesn't join in our chatter. We've grown so far apart. Perhaps she thinks I need her support or approval just like when I was a little girl.

"Dora, here's one of you in the swimming pool. Don't you look fantastic?"

The photo shows a smiling young woman with a great figure, looking straight into the camera and adopting a pose just like Esther Williams.

She doesn't say anything but comes over and sits down on the rug with us. For a while we continue looking at the photographs. Then she comes closer to me and puts her arm around my shoulders.

Lara smiles. It's a happy moment.

The housemaid says that tea is ready. The spell is broken.

Before we leave I asked her if I could have the photos and without a word she gives them to me. Now they're in our photograph albums at home in Jerusalem.

The Journey to Córdoba

I can't say for sure how old I was, eight or nine, I think, but I remember we left Buenos Aires very early in the morning when it was still all dark outside. We were going to Córdoba because my parents wanted to spend a few days in the mountains. Then suddenly the sun came up and it was dawn. It seemed to set the sky on fire.

One of my mother's sisters, Aunt Lisa, was traveling with us, and for once neither Ariel nor Dora were there.

It was a long journey but I remember I liked it. The hot, dry roads stretched out ahead of us. We had all the windows open and the air was so dry it burned.

We stopped on the way to cool down. The farther we drove from Buenos Aires, the emptier and sleepier the towns and villages we passed through became. Everywhere in the burning heat was quiet, the quiet of siesta time. The sun was amazingly white and its heat beat down on the whitewashed cement houses giving them a ghostly appearance. All the houses were the same: low, a single story, square and white, with small windows shuttered against the heat outside. A few colorless trees stood beside the houses and all around there was nothing but acres and acres of vast tracts of land. There seemed to be hardly any cars and the few we did see didn't look as though they were still capable of taking to the road. And yet, oddly, we did come across one service station. By then we urgently needed the bathroom but we didn't dare use the facilities at that place. Mosquitoes and other insects whined and buzzed around us but they weren't frightening. That was the first time I saw a centipede. Mamá explained to me what it was. She was fascinated by all insects. She would pick them up with her fingers and examine them closely. I wonder why she was a businesswoman if in reality it was scientific research that interested her.

Aunt Lisa smiled at everything. She was a very pretty woman. They all used to say she was very good-looking. She had such an easy way of walking, very straight-backed and elegant. She had a beautiful voice and loved singing. I used to admire the way she did her red hair. She would wind strands of it around pipe-cleaners and then when she took them out it made her hair all wavy. And she wore floral dresses made of some material that looked as though it came to life as she moved. Although she seemed very young to me she was actually older than my mother. Everyone felt sorry for her. Her husband had abandoned her, leaving her on her own to bring up four children. My grandfather didn't approve of divorce and so she lived alone for the rest of her life. But she didn't complain. She used to like listening to the radio in the evening. All her favorite programs were stories of love and despair. Aunt Lisa was always willing to help whoever needed her. Her house was so clean, it shone. In her kitchen there would always be a cake she had just baked and a cup of tea. Her balcony was like a small garden. The large window had crocheted curtains that she had made herself. My mother also knew how to crochet. I inherited from her a bedspread and a wool shawl for my first baby. I wrapped each of my daughters in that shawl when they were babies and I brought it out again for my grandson when he was born. For me, using that little shawl, it felt as though my mother was there. None of my sisters knitted or knew how to crochet. In fact, we'd so often heard our father say he didn't want to see any of his daughters knitting. I never understood why he said that.

In Córdoba I overheard my mother talking with my aunt. They were planning to go and see my aunt's husband who had abandoned her. To me, the idea seemed terribly romantic. Obviously, my mother nurtured the hope of an arrangement of some sort. My father in his panama, smoking a cigarette, was a little farther on, away from the car. He didn't say anything.

Juana, as usual, had her own version of it. Juana's eyes were the green of grapes and her mouth was thin-lipped. She was small and slight and disagreeable. She always seemed to be on the verge of tears. Anything made her cry. She'd be very quiet, not saying a word, but would watch everything that was going on around her. Pá and Má were always very protective of her and so was my eldest sister. I often heard my mother say, "Juana, that's enough of those crocodile tears." She would turn pale and her mouth became two tense lines.

"None of you understand me. I suffer because of all of you."

That's how Juana would respond. She was never a good student and always had problems with the teachers. She was intelligent but never found her way in life.

I was the strong daughter and she was the delicate, sensitive one and supposedly not in very good health. Much, much later I used to refer to her as the Lady of the Camellias.

I was as strong as a horse and certainly lacked any grace. My eldest sister referred to me as the one with heavy elephant feet.

Adela would spend ages in front of the mirror admiring herself. She was tall and slim and knew she was pretty. They all referred to her as the beautiful one of the family. She wore clothes like her favorite movie stars and copied their hairstyles. She loved Rita Hayworth and Ava Gardner. She would spend hours in front of that mirror, practicing different expressions and gestures, doing her hair and putting on makeup. She would walk around her bedroom so she could admire her reflection in the mirror. She went to art school and it was she who first instilled in me my love of art and gave me my first lessons on Rubens and the cherubs. I listened very attentively.

I liked the hotel we stayed at in Córdoba. It was almost at the top of a mountain, so high it seemed one could touch the stars. In Córdoba the stars were enormous, nothing like the small, insignificant ones we had in Buenos Aires. And the sky was different too. It was the deep blue color of the ink we used at school. Our new world had white walls, a red roof, and red-tiled floors that shone. The bedrooms were spacious. I shared mine with Juana. They would always put us together. She had first choice of the beds. The sheets were highly starched and cold. At night it was cold and beyond the window all you could see was darkness and shadows. Swaying in the wind, the trees seemed to be talking in whispers. Even now, it makes me shiver remembering those sighing trees at night. There were no street lights in the town. It was like being surrounded by an abyss. We were on another planet.

The accent of the local Córdoba people amused me. They spoke as though they were singing. It was certainly different and for people like us from the big city of Buenos Aires, these provincial people were proof of the distance we'd covered. They seemed primitive to those of us who were only used to the people living in the capital who had been influenced by French culture, were very conceited, and thought themselves all-powerful. The provinces versus the capital.

My mother didn't like anything. There were arguments from day one. I was afraid when things were like that and voices were raised. When that happened, all I wanted was to get away and cover my ears so I couldn't hear the shouting and the insults. My parents would shut themselves up in their room and then it would begin. My mother was a very jealous woman.

Mamá, when she was very young, was driven to despair at seeing her home filled with immigrants who had escaped from Europe. It seemed to her that they took up all the free space and all her parents' spare time. She didn't understand the language they spoke although her parents understood and spoke it perfectly. When they spoke in Spanish they had an accent that made her feel ashamed of them. My mother belonged to that young generation educated in Latin America who wanted to rid themselves of the memories of Europe where they had been badly treated, discriminated against, and sent to concentration camps. They brought to Buenos Aires a cultural heritage that within a very short span of time fused with the local *porteño* culture to create something not yet identifiable. Poetry reading at the Recoleta, loving Sarah Bernhardt and Paulina Singerman, not missing a single play by Sholem Aleichem or Chekhov that was performed in Yiddish, was their cultural lifeblood.

My maternal grandfather continued wearing his long black coat and his wide-brimmed black hat. His beard was white. He used to pray outside in the courtyard with his *tallit* around his shoulders. My mother didn't want her school friends to see him. He was too exotic for the young ladies who went to Colegio Bermejo. In the end, that school was the first to allow women to study business. Society wasn't that liberal then.

A photograph of my maternal grandfather hangs on the wall of my study in Jerusalem. I often look at it, trying to find the key that might help me understand what went on inside that white head of his with its meticulously trimmed beard. What were those deep-set, very blue eyes hiding? He was tall and slim and in the photograph he's wearing his black coat, his *kippa*, and his black and white *tallit*. I never knew him so he's a stranger to me. Everything I know about him I learned through stories the family used to tell. So I don't actually know what he was like, what he thought, how he felt about living in this new world so very different from the one he was born into and where he was educated. I don't think he ever spoke about that very much. In Argentina he never attained what he wanted. He had to look after his family of seven children—three boys and four girls. The boys grew into men who never worked because it was enough for them simply to flaunt the family name, which let them be welcomed into the homes of the most prestigious Jewish families in Argentina.

* * *

"Are we going to eat, Mommy?" the girls ask.

"Yes, my loves, I just get lost in my memories sometimes, but it's so wonderful to get back to you."

* * *

Mamá was complaining; we didn't have any clothes. It has been quite a while now since we'd gotten any new clothes. On Fridays the chicken is divided into small portions. María, the maid, quietly grumbles and the cooks don't stay with us for long. The Friday napkins are beginning to look threadbare and so are the collars of my father's shirts.

At my school they don't say anything. My parents warned me not to say a word against the President or the government and never to repeat outside the house anything I might have overheard the family talking about. There was censorship, a feeling of danger and therefore of fear. Juana came home with some stories sometimes but I knew that not everything my sister said was true. I know my sister lies sometimes.

Juana often daydreamed. In the family she was thought of as the poet with her green eyes looking at the world in a detached way. She was accepted by the best ballet school but our parents didn't want her to take ballet too seriously. Our aunts thought she was finer and more beautiful even than Leslie Caron, who was a favorite.

The photograph of the Presidential couple is displayed on all the walls and in all the streets. The school day begins with children writing in their exercise books:

Perón Cumple   Evita Dignifica.[3]

"Mamá, what does that mean?"

The reply just added another to the many replies I had been getting recently:

"Child, don't ask about it and don't talk about it. That's just the way it is and that's that."

One Saturday night I can remember clearly even what I was writing at the time. Juana was in her bedroom, listening to the radio. Papá, Mamá, and Adela had gone out. Then suddenly the program just stopped. A very deep, suave voice announced the death of Evita. It was 8:25 in the evening.

As with all events of historic importance or personal tragedy, I've since verified it, one fixes that moment just like a photograph that stays in one's mind forever. There are few who don't recall what he or she was doing when a loved one died or when the Twin

---

3 Perón Accomplishes, Evita Dignifies.

Towers were attacked and we watched and watched over and over again as though it were some nonstop horror movie as the planes came out of the sky and people threw themselves out of windows from such an awful height.

After that announcement, we weren't allowed to listen to the most popular programs on Radio El Mundo. But secretly we did, with the connivance of the maids, because they also liked those programs. We didn't have television then and people would huddle together to **listen** to the fifteen-minute broadcast that started at 7:30 in the evening: "*¡Qué pareja!*"[4] with Blanquita Santos and Héctor Maselli, then there was a musical interlude with "*Héctor y su jazz*,"[5] music I adored, and then later on there was "*El Glostora tango club*," and at 8:15 was the comedy serial we were all waiting for, "*Los Pérez García*." Evita's death interrupted our favorite program.

Juana came running into my room. "Gabriela, it's awful, what's going to happen now?"

"Why are you in such a state?"

"You don't understand. We have to be very careful. People loved her so much. Listen, can't you hear them shouting 'Santa Evita! Santa Evita!'?"

Thousands of people were crying and shouting in the streets. We didn't know what to do. We just waited for our parents to come home.

"Have you heard?" It was Mamá coming upstairs. She was very pale. Adela was following behind her and then Papá, who was quickly closing all the windows.

It was July 26, 1952.

---

4 "What a couple!"

5 "Héctor and his jazz"

We didn't leave the house for a whole week. There were incredible demonstrations of grief with thousands and thousands of people in the streets, some with candles and flowers, going to the funeral chapel.

My family didn't talk about the events much, not even on the phone. They just kept saying all the time, "What's going to happen now?"

During the months that followed Evita's death, there was a portrait of her hanging in our dining room. Every day the family and the staff would stand in front of it and observe a moment of silence. Whether in the street, at meetings, at the movie theater, or in shops, no one, absolutely no one, dared say anything. Terror reigned.

Radio programs were interrupted at the fateful hour and the suave voice of the announcer would intone, "It's twenty-five minutes past eight, the hour at which Eva Perón became immortal."

Meanwhile, the government began to fall apart. After a year of struggle, rumors started to circulate with growing evidence of orgies in the president's house. His predilection for young girls was a known fact but now there was even mention of girls under fifteen.

I quickly ran up the steps because María didn't like to be kept waiting. The marble steps had just been washed and they smelled nice. The table was set in the dining room. I was getting impatient for the school holidays to come to an end. School would be more fun at the moment. We hadn't gone anywhere over the holiday. Mamá said we'd be staying in the city this year.

"Gabriela," María was calling me. "There's a surprise for you. You're going out to a concert in the Centenario Park amphitheater this evening."

It was the Boston Symphony Orchestra conducted by Arthur Fiedler. I'll never forget that concert or the conductor's white hair that seemed to fly with every impassioned movement of his baton.

Going out at night, getting dressed up, listening to music—how wonderful!

"So I wanted to tell you the meal will be a quick one this evening."

"But where's Papá? Má, shall I help you get your evening bag ready?"

My mother looked at me; there was almost sadness in her eyes but those green eyes still managed a slight sparkle of excitement.

"Yes, of course you can, but don't put too much perfume on my handkerchief."

"Aren't you going to put on any jewelry?"

My mother looked at herself in the mirror and said, "No, it wouldn't be right for an open-air concert. It's not that formal."

Papá was smiling, looking at my mother's reflection in the mirror. It was just as well she'd said that as all the jewelry had been pawned. "Your mother looks lovely with or without any jewelry. Gabriela, come and help me with my cufflinks."

We climbed into the car and arrived at the amphitheater. The car was full of perfume and smiles. Pá and Má walked slightly ahead of three of their children. Arielito was away at the Residencia Johnson boarding school and my eldest sister was married. Pá's hair had gone very gray and he'd lost a lot of weight. Mamá looked very small beside him. That was why she always did her hair in a high hairstyle and wore high-heeled shoes. Papá laughed, gave her a kiss on the forehead, and called her his princess. In the interval we ate ice cream.

The most pertinent words that come to mind to describe that particular period are "whirlpool" and "vertigo." "Whirlpool" because everything started swirling and shifting. Because of the disorder, the accumulation of everything and the confusion around me. And "vertigo" because of how disturbing that confusion was. There was such a strong sensation of insecurity and fear that made us feel constantly as though we were on the edge of an unknown, deep, dark chasm. There was also the fear of doing or saying something that might be harmful to those you loved and send them falling into that abyss.

The following quotation seems so apt: "He who seeks to approach his own buried past must conduct himself like a man digging."[6]

* * *

We're going to travel north, to Salta and Jujuy. The suitcases are already packed and I am feeling rather anxious. When I was a young girl I only knew Tucumán because part of my family had settled in that province at the beginning of the last century.

My mother's elder sister had married a man who owned land there, far away, in the north. They used to say she wasn't very happy. It was because of her, Aunt Reina, that the family had to leave Russia in 1905. That was the year when Reina raised the red flag. They were a well-established family and fully aware of the danger there could be for Jews. My grandfather, Reina's father, was a secondary school teacher. He decided that the whole family—him and his wife plus all seven children—had to leave. They arrived in Buenos Aires four years later, in 1909. My aunt was an educated young woman and the husband they chose for her was a good man but very ordinary. He loved his wife very much and spoiled her. She found happiness in her children and her books. We used to call him the *gaucho* uncle. When he left his ranch and went to the city,

---

6 Walter Benjamin, *Berlin Childhood around 1900*.

after lunch he would meet up with the police officer of the district and they'd play chess together. Moreno, the Creole in his uniform, and the Jewish immigrant in his leather jacket and big, fair, almost white moustache, would move the chess pieces on the black and white board, pieces of history, of friendship and simply of life itself.

In the winter Juana and I would go visit Aunt Reina and her family. That part of the family is the one that suffered most under the military junta with persecution, terror, and death. My cousin Perla and her husband were combatants with the *guerrilleros*. They fought for ideals that never came to be.

The rest of the family disappeared after black crosses were painted on the doors of their house. It was a sign that meant they were marked, with no possible remission.

That branch of the family scattered. We had very little news of them and who had managed to survive. I know that my cousin Ernesto immigrated to Spain where he is a doctor. I haven't looked for him. If he has decided to remain silent about it all then I must respect that silence.

Having worked alongside those who have been ravaged by war or state terrorism, I know how strong the feelings of guilt are in those who survived both toward themselves and toward others. There are no words to describe that situation and the line running between memory and imagination is a tangle too difficult to unravel.

"To summarize, the poverty and deception of those below and the greed and voraciousness of those above create a poisoned, mined atmosphere that the army can scent: presenting itself as a defender of the poor and wronged, it leaves its quarters and reaches out to grab power."[7]

---

7 Richard Kapuscinski, Ébano.

Homework for Gabriela: When you have finished unravelling this two-colored skein of wool—because nothing is so black or so white as I thought it was when I was young—before it's too late you should send a friendly note to your cousin Ernesto, the *tucumano*.

There was a great difference in age between my mother and Aunt Reina because when Aunt Reina's first child was born my mother was only three.

In those days, people who lived in the provinces and had land or worked on the land never or very rarely traveled. If a person got engaged to someone from another town, there would be parties and then the young woman would go to visit the town where her fiancé lived. They would only see each other at weddings or funerals. A sign of rising up the social ladder was undoubtedly family reunions over the winter holidays.

So Mamá traveled by train for several hours to get to Santiago del Estero, one of the poorest provinces in Argentina. It became fashionable to spend a season at the Río Hondo spas. She would go there to meet Aunt Rosa. In the middle of a semi-desert they would go to the hot underwater springs. It was mostly people from the capital who went there, spending a few weeks in the winter at the colonial hotel in select company. Mamá talked about confidential things with her sister. We didn't know her sister. She lived too far away.

Papá, like many other bourgeois husbands of that generation, would come to join us but only for a few days at the end of our stay. He came to have a little rest and then accompany us back to the capital. I was always rather anxious about the train journey, imagining something like in a movie. The grown-ups would say they arrived tired and literally covered in dust.

Mamá usually went on her own to the spa. When she got back she would tell us that there was such poverty in the north that *campesina* peasants would give birth in the fields and abandon their babies in ditches because they couldn't feed them. Many waited for the "ladies" to arrive so they could ask them for a job. That's how, little by little, the shanty towns developed all around the capital.

Those stories made such an impression on me. I just couldn't understand why it was like that. Around that time a book was published denouncing the situation: *Villa miseria tambien es América* by Bernardo Verbitzky. I was a teenager then and devoured that book. It spoke of the highs and lows of the city of Buenos Aires. He described how in those agglomerations of cardboard, corrugated iron, and wood, there lived hundreds of thousands of people in Argentina. The shanty town of Villa 31 Retiro, bordering a stately railway station of the capital and one of its most affluent neighborhoods, was constantly growing, taking over more and more space with its ever-increasing population living in conditions of extreme poverty. It began in 1930 and now there are 70,000 people still living there in what are no more than shacks, living conditions there are deplorable.

The immigrants arriving in the capital were very different from those who arrived at the time as my grandparents. People now came from the north, from Bolivia, Peru, and Ecuador, and all of them fleeing poverty. They were distinguishable from the Creole by their indigenous features and the color of their skin. Although they spoke Spanish, their accent marked them as indigenous people from the mountains. They used Quechua words and phrases that weren't absorbed into local Buenos Aires speech.

Horacio Quiroga related magical tales about the people who lived as they'd always lived, completely closed off from modern society, in the Entre Ríos and Misiones jungle. His stories filled us with fear; even the title of his book made us shudder: *Cuentos de locura y de muerte*.[8]

The gulf between the capital and some of the provinces was enormous and it still is. The dreams of Che Guevara, that idol and indestructible icon of generations of Latin Americans, were never realized.

* * *

It is a bad landing when the plane touches down in Salta. Ayala is frightened and she looks very pale. She isn't the only one. A car is waiting to take us to the hotel.

It is an old colonial house that has been converted into a hotel. There are the typical colonial wrought iron bars over the windows, water butts, and antique mahogany furniture that makes us feel we have gone back a century. The marble staircase is majestic. We all think the high-ceilinged bedrooms, the linen sheets, and the enormous bathtubs are marvelous.

We take a walk around. It seems later than the time our watches indicate. The street lights are dim. The hotel is like an island, a Russian doll inside a far darker world. The meal is more than modest.

We get up very early the next morning and have breakfast. We are hungry. The bread is so fresh it is still warm from the oven.

The dining room is under a glass roof surrounded by gardens. We stay for longer than we intended around the breakfast table with its white crockery, the bright colors of the fruit and sweets, and the delicious smells of coffee and chocolate wafting around us. But the clear blue sky is beckoning us outside.

---

8 *Tales of Madness and Death*

The Journey to Córdoba

There is a group of seven of us in the minibus. There is one couple, she is Austrian and he Italian, both diplomats; a man with a small white beard who turns out to be a Spanish psychiatrist specializing in nothing less than love; and us four. We adopt the Spaniard. He observes my daughters. Noemia is the one to whom he gets closest. He leaves Lara, who is already married, to her research without asking her too many questions. Ayala looks for the right angles and light for her photos.

The scenery is majestic. The height of the mountains, the giant cactuses, and at each turn seemingly bottomless precipices. We are dumbstruck at the wonder of it all. We stop halfway along the mountain range. I climb up with my three daughters and I feel free. Touching, smelling, sweating, and feeling the challenge of nature and its demands on us, having to be constantly on the lookout for possible danger.

Lara climbs with a firm step. Ayala is looking back to see if I am following. Noemia and I stand for a while holding hands, then we went on. The red earth colors our skin.

* * *

"Gabriela, run, come here!" It was Papá's voice in the woods at Palermo. I must have been about five. I had had a very bad cough and they'd brought me out to the woods to breathe the clean morning air because that was when one could best smell the eucalyptus. Pá was running like a boy. He loved being out in the open air. I could see Mamá wearing her elegant brown coat with a fur collar and hat. She watched us happily. She didn't run around with us. She was not very fond of sports.

I ran to Pá who was waiting to catch me, his arms outstretched. He was laughing, laughing, and he called out, "Gabrielita, my Gaby, come here!" I jumped into his arms and he twirled me around. I was so happy.

Buenos Aires

"Mommy," Ayala is calling me, "I climbed up. Don't stay down there. Do you need some help?" Her voice brings me back from the tangle of dreams into the space where once we are awake we search to find meaning in the secrets of dreams and their confusion. There may be a similar reality but it's out of focus with the known images of another focal plane, yet between both images there are similarities and differences. The dream pales in significance on waking into the real world.

> I dreamed that I went back to the hotel. The town had no name. I tried hard to find out what it was but I couldn't. I don't know how long I was dreaming but where the hotel had stood there was now nothing but a pile of rubble. They told me it had been demolished because there had been a lot of trouble and they couldn't inform anyone. But where are my suitcases?

We look at it approvingly. Yes, something nice and hot, a room with lights and smiling voices—that's what we need to cut the thread of the past.

A place called Dandy had been one of my favorite cafés when I was young, very young. The sandwiches and hot toast at tea time were renowned.

"Was this one of the places you used to come to, Mommy?" Lara asks, looking at everything around her as she usually does.

"I can imagine you here very well, with your girlfriends, planning your weekend or your next tennis match. The club wasn't far away. Mía, how do you imagine Mommy was?"

They start to describe me. They invent clothes for me, imitate my voice, my gestures, and my remarks.

What has happened? Yes, it's true they've been "reading" me over these weeks we've been together. Is it possible I've managed to paint this younger version of myself for them? To paint the girl I used to be? They're talking amongst themselves as though I'm not there.

* * *

It was barely dawn and it was winter. The doctor had said I should have a blood test. Papá woke me up early and we went in the car. I can remember they gave me a sidelong glance. They were afraid I was going to cry. I didn't cry. I was thinking about what I had been promised—Papá would take me to Águila, the best confectioner's in town, to have milk coffee and croissants. I loved those privileged moments. I went there many other times. The last time was when my father accompanied me to my appointment for a blood test to confirm I was expecting. That time they did a blood test on him too. He didn't tell me but he was already ill. He died three years later.

* * *

We land in Puerto Gallegos but don't get off the plane. We are flying south, way south, over the Argentine Pampas. Looking out of the small window we can see endless land stretching out all around us. It seems the airport is lost in the midst of such immensity.

"This country is so vast," Mía says. "Israel is so small you can fly from north to south in under an hour!"

"We've been traveling for four and a half hours already and we still haven't arrived," Lara says. "It seems like there's no one living here; where are all the people?"

I wonder where all the Indians are, the people belonging to this land, this magic Patagonia.

The air currents make it a very rough, bumpy flight. I can feel Ayala's hand is sweaty and cold. Lara is biting her nails while she reads a scientific article and Noemia is drawing, glancing at Ayala every now and then.

* * *

Ayala, our third daughter, was born in Jerusalem on a Sunday in August, one of those days of oppressive Mediterranean heat. When I felt the first labor pains I called my husband, not my mother. Howard was waiting outside, reading a small prayer book my father had given him.

Ayala's birth was induced. They kept her in the hospital for three days because she was born with jaundice. During her first few months everything seemed fine.

We lived in Mexico City for three years. Howard taught at El Colegio de México and I was at the Iberoamericana. Noemia was born there. My father died and at his graveside I promised him I would finish my doctorate.

Noemia began walking at sixteen months. We were on the train traveling from Helsinki to Rovaniemi, in Finland's Arctic region. She has a strong character and makes decisions on her own. No-one knows anything about her problems until they have been solved. She has such a very gentle voice that sometimes we can't hear her. Howard says that in whatever language she speaks, she speaks with a Polish accent. She began to read later than Lara did and I was worried. Now she's the one who helps me with Israeli literature.

* * *

"Gabriela, how are you getting on with *Uncle Tom's Cabin?*" Mamá asked.

We were in the car one Sunday night on our way back from the *quinta*. I din't answer. I could feel Juana's inquisitive, mocking stare.

"I didn't read much of it. I was doing other things," I replied.

"Playing, running around, and looking for trouble," Juana added.

"I was asking Gabriela, not you," Mamá retorted.

I had been saved. This once, anyway.

I continued looking out the car window at the lights inside the houses we passed by. I wanted to imagine what they were like inside. Did the people who lived there also ask their children how many pages of *Uncle Tom's Cabin* they had read?

Who would ever have thought that I'd have a doctorate in Comparative Literature? I can't remember making any plans for a professional career. I thought about getting married at some point but I wasn't at all confident about my looks or ever falling in love with anyone.

* * *

"I've already asked you, where can we find a good lunch and not in a place that's just for tourists? Come on, I'm hungry." Ayala is getting impatient.

* * *

The doctor told me to leave her be, that babies eat when they're hungry. She wasn't walking or talking.

I began to worry but they reminded me that my other daughters had also been late developers. "Be patient, don't get hysterical, please," they repeated over and over again.

I was called all different sorts of names but particularly one of being guilty because I didn't know how to cook properly and because I worked and didn't spend enough time with the children.

When she was four, thanks to the English nanny we had, Ayala began walking. I told myself, well, she'll do everything at her own pace.

Ayala didn't chew her food and she would get annoyed when I wanted to give her anything other than a bottle. She was more than two years old by then. But sometimes she would eat a small piece of cake.

We moved to Paris. Howard had a very interesting job and I had thought of doing a postgraduate course with Roland Barthes, but in March 1980, he was knocked down by a car and killed as he crossed the street. French intellectuals mourned the loss of their semiologist.

My plans of continuing my studies also came to a halt that day on that street.

When Ayala was four she still hardly talked at all. We took her to therapists and specialists. Finally a neurologist diagnosed minor damage affecting the left side of the brain.

Her struggle continues, even to this day. She has made incredible progress. She has a fighting spirit. Today—she is now in her thirties—her problem isn't apparent. Her strong points are sculpture and writing…facing off.

"Yes, you're right, let's go and have lunch now. It's past two o'clock."

"Look, there's a dog!" Mía and Ayala run toward it. They can't resist saying hello to every dog they come across.

Ayala did veterinary studies and Mía takes home any dog she thinks is a stray. Then when the dogs' owners come around, she questions them in such detail to see if they are really worthy of having a dog, which is definitely the best animal there is as far as she's concerned.

"Look, Mommy, he's so cute!" Both girls look so happy while the dog, front paws in the air, surrenders to their pats and strokes.

The air is becoming whiter. We are beginning to feel how close we are to the glaciers. We ask if we're following the right path and they tell us "*la cocina*," the restaurant, isn't far ahead and that they'll still be serving lunch when we get there. That welcome information spurs us on.

A very different, unexpected scene greets us. There's a most unusual mixture of something Creole and German together with appetizing smells of Italian sauces.

On the walls are gaucho souvenirs, photos of Bavaria and the enormous Munich beer halls that can accommodate a thousand people, and cloves of garlic hanging from the chimney. An old iron stove stands in the center of the dining room. It's where they slice the bread. It's identical to the one my parents had in our country house.

The waitress is fair with blue eyes. I can't help asking her where she's from.

"My family came from Germany," she answers rather reluctantly.

I don't ask her any more questions because I can see my children's faces begging me not to say any more about it.

The whole region of the south of Argentina and Chile and also Paraguay were known meeting points for Nazis who escaped after World War II. The second generation shouldn't be judged. That's how it should be and yet even now that doctrine is still admired and celebrated by many of the descendants of those exiles.

We now know that many Nazi war criminals and prominent Italian fascists were granted special protection by the government of Juan Domingo Perón, who had done his military studies in Berlin in the 1930s and later in Italy and showed his fervent support for Mussolini. A very sad ideological combination for a people's government. It explains the hotbed of nationalistic and anti-Semitic associations that shamelessly flourished in Buenos Aires at that time.

Who could have forgotten Gabriela, Gabriela Sirota, the young Jewish student on her way to class who was attacked, kidnapped, and tortured by young men from Tacuara's ultra-nationalist group in the 1960s?

They burned her body with cigarettes and they tattooed a swastika on her chest with knives. And Saudi Arabia's representative to the United Nations congratulated Tacuara on its "crusade against Zionism."

The meal, especially the pasta, is delicious, and we enjoy it with some excellent wine.

We leave the restaurant happy and slightly tipsy. We start walking along the boulevard intending to buy some presents to take back home. There aren't many shops open but one in particular catches our attention. It sells not only the usual tourist souvenirs of fleece slippers, postcards, *matés*, and sweets, but also music and books. A very good-looking woman greets us with a large smile. The place is spacious and colorful.

I begin looking at the books. The woman puts on some tango music. I look at her and ask, "Would you like to dance?" The woman looks at me. She is of medium height and probably of Italian origin with her dark eyes, olive skin, and sensual mouth. She is dressed in a brown tweed skirt and matching blouse, and her nails are unpolished. She is wearing moccasins and opaque tights. Ah, my mania for detail! She probably comes from the north of Italy. We look at each other and there seems to be recognition. We're both daughters of migration, Europe, famine, and war destroying that continent.

We begin dancing in the shop. My daughters circle around us. I am taken back to the time when they nicknamed me "Horse" because my movements were slow.

"You haven't forgotten how to tango. You dance well."

The girls are clapping.

We buy CDs, postcards, books, and sweets. As we are leaving the shop, I say, "Thank you, sister, you've given me a wonderful present."

I feel better than ever.

Accepting both the past and the present is something miraculous. She says goodbye to me: "Enjoy your family. Your daughters are really wonderful."

* * *

"Má, Gabriela shouldn't come. No one asks her to dance. They say she's like a broomstick."

We had just come back from the beach and Juana was getting ready to go to a party. I was in the bathroom and I could overhear her talking to my parents. I kept listening. I was surely the most scorned member of the family, a teenager growing like a weed, and I felt like a match ready to be set alight with the slightest spark.

"I don't want to go anyway, Juana, I want to get up early because I have a tennis game in the morning."

The following day I played tennis happily. I looked at the others as though they were strangers to me, which in fact was true. I didn't know them and they didn't know me.

* * *

"Mommy, it's lovely. You've really got the rhythm. Tango fits you like a glove. And best of all is seeing you so happy," Lara says.

"Thank you, Lara, if you only knew…that was almost like breaking a taboo…dancing, and in Argentina! Did you know that I only began to dance when I arrived in Israel? I could only do it once I'd overcome my complexes about my figure and lack of gracefulness, things that always hung over me because of my sisters and their constant criticism."

They start laughing. "You had complexes? Tell us, we want to know all about them," Ayala says.

* * *

I came back from the office. The house was all quiet. I opened the door to Lara's bedroom. She was writing and chewing gum. She had put a pile of gum beside her on the desk.

"Hi, Mommy, I'm just going to finish this and then I'll come."

She went on writing. She was always writing something.

"Where are the others?"

"Dressing up as usual. What else would they be doing?"

The bedroom door was closed. I could hear voices inside. I went in and surprised them. Noemia and Ayala were all dressed up with masses of makeup. They had emptied my wardrobe and were an absolute sight to behold. They threw themselves around on my bed with peals of laughter. I threw myself on top of them and hugged them. They were so wonderful!

* * *

We arrive in Calafate and the cold, white, clear air hits us full in the face. It wakes us up.

The streets are wide and the houses have red roofs. Men are walking around wearing jackets in all colors of the rainbow. We don't say anything but just look and absorb it all.

There is an obvious influence of German traditions here with the city's whole structure, its architecture, and the gardens. I'm struck by unbidden memories of fears my parents transmitted to me about the war and Argentina's alignment with the axis—Rome, Berlin, Tokyo, and Buenos Aires—and the rumors about the preparation of concentration camps in Entre Ríos.

"Here it is, Señora, we've arrived."

Wood Anemones at Tea Time

The hotel is built of stone and wood. Through the main door we can glimpse a warm, golden light. It looks welcoming.

"It's beautiful, Mommy. Look at the color of the wood," Mía says.

It's the color of her eyes—honey and mahogany.

The crackling fire in the grate, the wooden walls and ceiling, the comfortable sofas just inviting us to sit down with a book and a cup of tea to enjoy the coziness of the place. Tables are covered with damask cloths, folding doors open onto a billiard room, and enormous windows look out at the boundless landscape beyond.

This time it's Lara's turn to share my room. She leaves her suitcase and goes down to reception to ask if they have Internet. She wants to write to her husband, who's in London.

"I want to send some email as well," shout Noemia and Ayala in unison.

I unpack. I want to have a look around the town and then eat.

We go to bed early, each of us with our own collection of emotions. Excluding Howard from this journey means I have stopped the children from seeing me as a wife.

I have to, I must do it alone, without his support. I must paint this picture with colors that are mine and mine alone. I'm actually doing it for us. The fact that I canceled the trip to the waterfalls in order to shorten the journey and spend more time with him. My reconciliation with the girl I once was and the different facets of my character now—I feel this process is essential if I want to keep breathing. Howard, perhaps I'll make this same journey with you one day, but first I must do it with my daughters. They're my hardest, clearest judges. It's an essential part of my legacy: what Gabriela is like, what she used to be like, and how they read her. Yes, Howard, I miss you, but now is not the time for me to hold your hand or rest my head on your shoulder.

I draw the curtains. I can see Lara's silhouette, her delicate profile, and I listen to the breathing of my firstborn. She radiates peace and confidence. The grail I'm striving to attain in this crusade is to have confidence. For brief fits and starts that feeling seems slightly less unattainable.

I'll email Howard tomorrow. Now I must sleep and catch my breath so I can continue watching this shadow theater where the characters keep moving faster and faster inside the original kaleidoscope.

* * *

"Hi, Roberto, is this seat free?"

"Yes, you can sit there. Gabriela, let me introduce you to Howard."

We were in the Hebrew University of Jerusalem cafeteria. I didn't pay much attention to the new arrival, who frankly didn't seem very elegant.

"Gabriela, the books I let you borrow are actually Howard's."

"Oh! You're the one who has them then." He looks at me fixedly. "Look, I need them. Give me your address and I'll drop by and pick them up."

He came for his books and we've been together ever since.

* * *

It's a very small group of us with absolutely no experience, climbing the glacier. We take photos and no one says if they are frightened or if they have any doubts about this adventure.

We go in a small boat. They supply us with climbing boots and crampons. One more coffee and we set off to face this new challenge.

Noemia is climbing behind the guide. She's telling him about her knee trouble and the piece of metal that had been inserted when she damaged her knee dancing to rock music. She was studying at Cambridge when it happened. A very elegant way to get injured! We often pull her leg about it, about how she managed to find a very elegant way to injure her knee.

Ayala, Lara, and I follow them. Climbing with us are four other people and four guides. We very soon hear a tremendous rending sound; it was almost deafening. They tell us that it was a piece of the glacier breaking away, which apparently is something that happens regularly.

All around us, there is nothing but this massive, terrifying bulk of ice. It feels so powerful. It's so tremendous it's impossible to describe. All I can remember is whiteness as far as the eye can see and the loss of any feeling of reality. Quite hypnotizingly beautiful.

"We'll stop here for a while," one of the guides says. "From this point on it becomes much more difficult."

We have been walking for two hours.

"We have a good hour's walk ahead of us. Don't feel bad if you want to go back now. One of us can go with you. So who wants to go back and who wants to keep going?"

Ayala is the first to say she wants to continue. Mía and Lara cheer and I agree to keep going as well. The rest of the group is also coming with us.

It's true, it isn't easy but it is worth the effort.

"What I could do with now is a strong drink," one woman in the group says.

Half an hour later, one of the guides surprises us and says, "Is this what you wanted?" There in front of us is a wooden table with an array of whisky, ice, glasses, and chocolate. Seeing the ice displayed like that makes us laugh. All of us, almost without realizing it, for no other reason than that we are actually here, we laugh so much, almost hysterically. Lara, Noemia, and Ayala are taking photos near the precipice where we have stopped. Ayala, incredibly brave, is balancing on one leg in order to get some spectacular shots. I've learned to keep my fear to myself so as to bolster her self-esteem.

If I had seen it in a Buñuel or David Lynch movie I'd have thought, *How fantastic!* But the scene is in front of me, Gabriela, and my daughters and the others who, just like us, are looking for something beyond their normal existence. The elation we all feel is because we have found that something. Celebrating our find merited more than a whisky.

Inside me, I'm feeling the truth of that popular Chinese proverb: Descending is more difficult than ascending.

There isn't any talking; we simply listen to the rhythmic noise of our boat's keel on the blinding white ice, pushing so as not to slip. At the foot of Perito Moreno we leave the boats and sit down under the big trees that seem to want to protect us from the heavy drops of rain that have begun to fall.

The dark-room of memory has been enriched with new images to sparingly reveal when it overcomes sadness with no better reason than putting them in order in an album titled "Victory for Life."

We can't stop looking at the giant in front of us, and just there, where this morning our small boat had been, there's a block of ice about to fall into the water. The noise is tremendous, indescribable. We all stand up, petrified, smothering an outburst of cries, caught between fear and respect for the tremendous force of that giant block of ice that has separated from the glacier.

Back at the hotel, a hot shower helps us to talk about what we feel. It has been a very strong experience, one we will treasure.

* * *

My parents had cabin trunks. They would travel with them. They were very big and opened like an upright book with drawers and clothes hangers. They used to make lists of what they needed to pack. I would watch the whole procedure and sometimes I was entrusted with some task of the operation.

I think my life is shut up in different cabin trunks. And now I'm beginning to find the keys and know my secrets before rust and vermin get to them.

* * *

"Are we eating at the hotel tonight?"

The three girls are busy with their email. They all nod their heads.

When they join me in the dining room I'm already situated with a glass of wine. There's a bottle on the table and three other glasses.

"Were you frightened when that block of ice broke away from the glacier?" Noemia asks me. She's always so direct.

"Yes, but I was also fascinated by it and I'm happy to have experienced all that with you."

"Why?" Ayala wants to know.

"You know better than anyone, Ayala. Because we need to prove to ourselves what we're capable of doing, what I now call facing off."

"Yes, but was it dangerous or not?" insists my scientist daughter.

"Yes, perhaps. But in many ways this whole journey is also dangerous. We know that."

"We're not judging you, we're discovering a different you, a new you," Lara says. She looks straight at me with those green eyes of hers. Her look is so clear, she's facing up to me. Like I've been doing all this time. I'm facing up to things.

It's a very powerful moment. I don't want it to be over. I think of my own story and if only I could have had such complete moments with my mother at least once. How much we would have learned about each other!

"So you don't think I'm taking undue risks?" I ask.

"Yes, but I admire you for it. You want us to know about the different facets beyond 'the mother.' Thank you for having confidence in us and let's drink to Mamá!"

They all three raise their glasses to me. Confidence, having and giving confidence.

It's an almost limpid sky when we wake in the morning. We're going out to the Pampas. We're dressed in thick sweaters, jeans, and boots for our trip to the area where the "Las Violetas" ranch is located.

The endless landscape stretches out ahead of us. The land is flat, sparse, with only a few small houses. The road is dry and there is almost no vegetation.

* * *

It was December. Fidel Castro was visiting Buenos Aires. The whole city became electrified. Young people were getting ready to march and hail him as a great leader. The workers wanted to demand rights. The bourgeoisie watched and waited. I was with my group of school friends and we were excited, hoping to catch at least a glimpse of the man so covered in myth and mystery.

* * *

"Did you have left-leaning ideas at the time of Che?" Lara asks me.

I don't know if my ideas were to the left but I did have Socialist ideas and that was because in my parents' house there was always talk about Israeli society and the kibbutz system. To my mind, that seemed to be an ideal world where everyone had work, was educated, and everything was shared. I know that seems rather idyllic nowadays but those were the very bases on which the State of Israel was founded.

Grandfather David was a strong Zionist and he had taken part in the setting up of the first support centers in Palestine. He's buried in Jerusalem. When the Balfour Declaration happened in 1917, it was at his house that the important members of the community congregated.

"But Che, isn't that what he wanted? For everyone to have work, be educated, and share everything?" Ayala asks.

"Yes, certainly, those were his ideals, but then he imposed certain strictures. Of course anyone who wants to succeed needs to have discipline but they also need recognition of their personal needs and the most important is for that person to feel responsible through his or her own freedom. Self-effacement can't be a permanent condition. Dictatorship and indoctrination demand that a person not consider him or herself an individual. Small slaves must obey and if they're clones, then all the better. Behind them, from a platform, the nomenclature, the apparatchik, condemn, judge, or remove from office however they wish. With Che, his ideas were different and so that's why he came to an end."

"Do you still consider yourself to be politically to the left, a woman committed to and fighting for peace?" Lara wants to know.

"Yes, I do. I hope I'll always be able to defend my freedom of speech, freedom to write, and above all freedom of thought. If you destroy people's minds and their rights then you're destroying mankind."

Then Noemia asks me, "Why did you leave Argentina? Why didn't you do what your sisters did? I'm trying to understand but I'm not sure if I'm on the right track."

They're looking at me. It's the moment of truth. This is why I thought of doing this journey in the first place. And one by one, all those fragile onion skins are beginning to peel off. What should I tell them? What have I really found out?

"Then came the time to leave. To exiled lands and far-off deserts we were obliged to go as the gods' prophesied" (*The Aeneid*).

I've never understood very well why the gods' prophecies were disguised as plagues and embodied in wars, famine, and tyranny.

* * *

"Pá, Marina is traveling to Europe. She's going with two other girlfriends and her aunt. I want to go with them. It will only be for six weeks. They're going to Paris, Madrid, Rome, and London. Pá, I need to, I want to know those places."

My father was sitting at his desk at the factory. The noise of the machines was the sound that meant there was work and that the period when everything was closed up was now over. My father was trying to rebuild his business after all those years of dictatorship and lack of aluminum and steel.

"Gabriela, I understand that you want to travel, but where do you want to go? Is six weeks away from here all you're looking for? Think about it. What do you really want?"

He was right. What did I want? Just that trip with my friends or did I want something else?

"I could go and study in London."

"No, not London." Papá is categorical. "If you want to travel, then go to Jerusalem. Your ancestors, your grandparents would have been so proud and happy if they knew one of my daughters was following in their footsteps a hundred years later."

I suddenly felt a complete mixture of fear and surprise.

"The Hebrew University of Jerusalem, do you think? Really? If you let me go then I could…"

We looked at each other and laughed together.

"Yes, Gabriela, if you decide to go there then I'll support your decision. But you'll have to convince your mother and that won't be easy. Somehow I was waiting for you to ask if you could go there."

I left for Israel on the *Theodor Herzl* on March 6, 1964. No, I didn't run away, but what I'm sure of is that I had to go. I had to construct my own person without being annoyed by things and people around me. Today I have returned; I had come back before but never with my daughters. I need this return to my roots to know exactly who I am now and also I want to try and find out if I've disappointed the person I was back then when I took the boat to Israel. It's through my three daughters that I hope to find the answer.

I know intuitively the luck of having this trio say to me in unison, "Mamá, one should never forget one's past nor be ashamed of it."

Silently, I say to myself, *No, no I don't want to forget anything. I know who I am and what I have done.*

"Mommy," Ayala says, "when you gave us those small trunks to keep our special mementos in, you filled one for yourself, didn't you?"

Ayala, my Ayala, how is it that you always manage with so few words to reveal the whole?

Our stay gives us the time we need for long walks, for riding, for ice-covered lakes, solitude, and beautiful dawns.

Incidentally, we don't talk anymore about my troublesome departure. They talk about what they are feeling in this desolate land where the cries of the Indians massacred by General Roca still resound, about the gaucho with his guitar who stirs up images of the past, and the woman with skin so dry and wrinkled, kneading bread with her strong, firm hands. Yes, she is bound to keep believing in the future. The country is afraid of losing its soul. The people don't want the whole area to be turned into a theme park where tourists stare strangely at them and pay them a few coins to take their photograph.

Back in Calafate once more and we're off to the airport. I can't hide a strange feeling when we leave this clear, white landscape. It's doubtful we'll be here together again like we are today, which is now yesterday.

We're flying to the north, to Salta and Jujuy, two border provinces. On one side is Chile and farther to the north is Peru. There is still a very marked Indian influence, not merely in people's ways but also in the architecture, the food, the music, and above all in their features. There hasn't been as much intermarrying among the different ethnicities as there has been in other parts of the country. Northerners show the Indian pride at having survived persecutions and have kept as far as possible the pride of their race. The women's clothes are still the same as we can read about in history books and their language, although it is Spanish, retains much of their own dialects.

The captain announces that we're about to land. There is such tension in the cabin one can cut it with a knife.

"Ayalita, my pretty one, we're landing now."

She doesn't answer me. I'm afraid she's going to be sick. She isn't but nor is she smiling. Finally we touch down and rush off the plane. The runway is almost invisible. They have lit it with lamps. We collect our suitcases in silence. Noemia goes with her sister to the bathroom. Lara helps me with all the luggage. We find the driver who is waiting for us and Ayala comes out of the bathroom looking very white.

"My head hurts."

"You'll see, have a shower, wash your hair, brush your teeth, and afterward you'll feel fine again."

They know that's my remedy for most problems.

The provincial city has developed unevenly. One part of it is still colonial while the other strives to be modern.

"The lights are odd. They look as though they're about to go out all the time. Why?" Lara wants to know.

"It's the lack of energy. It's not just the people here but the things as well could do with a dose of vitamins." I try to give an ironic reply but don't quite pull it off.

The hotel is magical. It's very old with gardens and flat-stoned pathways. The whole building is white. The floors are red tiles and shining. There's an enormous fireplace, dark wooden furniture, and thick rugs.

"Welcome," they greet us at reception.

A world of bygone days that still lingers on, a world of a certain fragment of land-owning Argentine aristocracy.

My daughters look at the maids who seem to glide in their black uniforms with starched, lace-trimmed cambric aprons and white caps.

North Against South was the title of a book by Jules Verne that I read when I was a child. What will the world of the middle be like?

"Can I sleep in your room tonight?" Ayala asks. No one says she can't. She still looks so pale.

The room has a high ceiling, the sheets are starched, the towels are huckaback, the bathtub is enormous, and the windows overlook the gardens.

"Mommy, it's beautiful. It's just like in one of the chapters of *One Hundred Years of Solitude*,"[9] Lara says when she sees the adjoining room.

We go downstairs. It seems more like going into some family's private home than a hotel lounge. Silverware is shiningly displayed all around. We ask where we should go to eat. We say we don't want to go to a tourist venue but a place where local people eat.

In the end we get the information we want but not without a certain reluctance, probably because they wonder if I am being serious or perhaps they think such a venue wouldn't be suitable for us.

We get to the restaurant and order *salteñas*. No one who boasts of ever having tried them would dare to call them *empanadas* but

---

9 A novel by Gabriel García Márquez.

simply the name of where they come from: Salta, so they're called *salteñas*. I remember someone once telling me how to obtain that unique flavor. They said I had to be very careful about the harmony of what went inside, to be sure about choosing onions of just the right green, the yellow and white of the egg, and that the reds of the pepper and the meat shouldn't taint each other, I was warned. As though it were possible for just any old person to reproduce that delicacy!

The night is warm and the sky full of stars. The broad avenue with its hundred-year-old trees guides us back to the hotel.

* * *

Papá's factory was in La Boca.

"Look, Mommy, the name is still printed over the entrance."

Yes, that's all that's left now. A name half obliterated by time.

The houses are a single story, painted in every color possible. Most of the population consists of immigrants from Genoa in Italy and they say that the fishermen used to let them have leftover paint from their fishing boats and that's how the houses first came to be painted like that. The streets are paved and tango music so loved by tourists floats out from bars and restaurants. But it's easy to see the area is still a working-class district.

It's here that in 1536 the first Buenos Aires was founded.

Boca was shaped by the painter known as Quinquela Martín, an artist whose neo-impressionistic style reflected everyday life among the people living around the port. They also tell you with pride that it was there, in 1905, that America's first socialist delegate was elected—Don Alfredo Palacios.

"Pathway that once was bordered with clover and flowering reeds, a shadow you'll soon be, a shadow like me."

The song simply came to me, inevitable humming deep down inside me, in this small street of life where many would like to return and yet they cannot find the way nor find the strength to do it. But I did. That's enough of reproaches and regrets. As for the grand avenue, it takes less than ten minutes to go right down it.

"Má, was it here they threw in the '*desaparecidos*' as history calls them, during the dictatorship?"

"Yes, Noemia, here or farther on. The precise location doesn't change the magnitude of that horror. They took them in helicopters, still alive, after torturing them, and hurled them into the water. They called it 'being transferred,' like the Nazis before them who had all sorts of euphemisms to refer to the unimaginable."

They look at me, startled; their eyes show sadness.

What should I say to them? I was lucky enough not to be in the country at the time. Everything I heard about it came from friends and acquaintances who suffered under that dreadful regime and even some who adhered to it.

"Noemia, if you're interested, I can get you books and movies on the subject."

"All this, it still affects you, doesn't it."

How could it not keep affecting me, when ever since I was born I'd heard the names the Creoles call the minorities, over and over again: *gallego*, *ruso* (for Jew), *tano* (for Italian), *chino*, *negro*, and always followed by the contemptuous *mierda*. That's where we all come from, so why is there so much shit in this country's mouth? *All have been victims.*

Thinking about the world after each defeat—of law, of people, and of life itself—is more than arduous, it's a Herculean task. "Through me, people will fear death no more, I have made blind

Hope live among them." Times so dark as those Argentina went through make me doubt the promise of Aeschylus.

I have to make myself go down to the street this noisy *porteño* morning, so full of contrasts.

"You know what? Let's go and visit the museum dedicated to Evita. Does that sound like a good idea?"

When Evita died I remember the whole country was in mourning for several weeks. The streets were empty and on the radio the only music they broadcast was funereal or classical. And before then, because it became impossible to import aluminum, Papá's factory had to close down. The workers had to be dismissed. Although he had no work to do, my father would still get up early every day and go through what had been his daily routine: calisthenics, bath, *maté*, breakfast. Then he would get dressed and go to the office as usual as though everything had to keep a trace of normality.

Over the days of official mourning, which lasted for a month, my father didn't go out to the office. I think he didn't want people in the street to see that lights were on in the office or to hear that someone was answering the telephone. The days that followed her death it rained incessantly. The street lamps were covered with black crêpe. National mourning for a month was decreed and also the obligation to show one was in mourning. The front page of the daily papers was printed with a black border. People in the street wore wide mourning bands on their sleeves.

The vigil lasted twelve days under the dome of the Ministry of Labor. Half a million people kissed the glass lid of the coffin. People waiting to see her had to stand in line for up to ten hours in the rain and yet the line was endless. The staff at home were, of course, given permission to go and pay their respects.

Today I look with incredulity at what can happen, what fear can lead to when people are contaminated by a tyrannical regime.

We also put a photograph of Evita in the dining room with black crêpe paper across it. Before lunch, the family and the staff would stand in front of that photograph and there would be a moment of silence.

If I need to describe what I was like then, I see myself as a bookworm. I can remember odd sentences from some books, the stories of others, and some of them it's the paper they were printed on or the smell of their pages that come back to me.

"Here we are, Señora. Is it the first time you've been here?" The driver interrupts my risky digression.

With no further ado he launches into a complaint, one long diatribe. He speaks of Perón's legacy as an endemic ill, a mark that is indelible, even half a century later: "My children luckily managed to get Spanish citizenship and now they're there. I want them to study. For my wife and me, it's too late now."

In a quiet street in the Palermo district. In an old colonial-style house is the museum dedicated to Evita Perón.

The museum is cold, clean, and very tidy. There are many photographs, some papers, plenty of propaganda, and as far as I am concerned the whole place is less than mediocre. The tourist guides say the restaurant is very quiet. In fact those guides tell us how we should be looking at everything and they tell us the story with multicolored brushstrokes so as to remove any jagged edges and thus avoid any disagreeable surprises.

The Evita myth swelled with first the musical and then the movie in which Madonna played the leading role. The Perón movement is still perpetuated today through decades of populist philosophy and praxis that were there at the outset and now are a blank stamp vote provider.

If the girls ask me now what I'm feeling with all this in front of me, with so many wasted lives and political plans, I'll say I honestly don't know.

When they ask me again why I'm making this journey when my treasure of memories is deep inside me, before setting out my reasons I'll say we're doing it because I believe in filling in the gaps and settling debts. It's more than a valid reason for making this journey together, within my own specific geography.

* * *

Several claps of thunder tell us there is a storm on the way. The wind tears at the dead leaves on the trees and makes them whirl around. Will the trees be driven to despair by the unstoppable movement of the branches that end up being torn from the tree trunks that were holding them prisoner? It's clear that if we don't trim the branches we can't recreate. If we remain inhibited, mediocrity will take over. We must keep fighting to detach ourselves, the branches are crying out. Am I crying out too? The cars are shiny with the heavy rain falling and people are moving shadows trying to dodge the lightning. The drumming sound of the constant rain against the windows wakes me up. I look around me. Was I dreaming?

Everything, or almost everything comes back to me. I get up, go to the kitchen, and prepare some coffee. The window is awash with rain; it's like a thick, opaque curtain. Paris is gray and soundless. The water boils. I find a cup, look for the coffee, and the smell makes me think of Jerusalem and the market where I do my shopping on Thursdays.

The orchids have come into bloom. In Argentina it used to be a very special flower, expensive and extremely rare. People only gave orchids on very special occasions. I didn't use to like them. They looked artificial to me, as though they didn't have their own lives but were just a mark of ostentation. I like them now though, maybe because with time they have become popular or maybe because I have one just as I would have any other plant. I get excited when every now and then it produces a new flower.

Nowadays I become emotional far more than I used to. Tears come to me more often. Sometimes it bothers me but other times I just let them fall and it does me good.

I must make an effort to get back to the dream and confront my wrinkles—by that I mean my past and all its lengthy internal commentaries.

That dream wasn't a nightmare. The tears I felt when I woke were real. And so is my need to travel back to my own roots accompanied by my daughters. I go back through streets, houses, woods, the sea, and the mountains. I tell them about everything and they listen. Sometimes we laugh but we speak little.

I can feel the coffee cup warming my hands. It's talking to me and asking me questions. I'm trying to see my reflection in the last drops of coffee in the bottom of the cup. It's telling me, demanding me to…I'm telling myself to face up to it. Give life and truth to what's facing me. The most difficult thing in all of this is accepting it and loving it.

My husband is still asleep. He goes to bed late. He's one of those people who works best at night. They're inspired by the silence of the sleeping world around them. Whereas I feel I need to get washed and then drink my coffee while I get ready for a new day. I need another cup of coffee.

I don't realize the water's running and the coffee pot overflows. I'm looking at myself in the mirror in the kitchen.

What a waste of water. I wouldn't let that happen in Jerusalem. We live with constant reminders that the land is arid and we must therefore save water. When I'm there I always have only a very quick shower. When I'm in Paris I hesitate before having a proper bath because the need to save water stays with me even when I'm in a land where there's plenty.

It's still raining. I open the window and the wind hits me full in the face. I like feeling the cold air and knowing that if I close the window, not only will the house be warm but even the walls will protect me.

I straighten my back. I listen to the instructions my mother used to give us but now it's different. I feel fine.

They say we need to build our own backbone. That it's our internal pyramid. During my journey I am trying to build it, thinking that when I reach the top I will find the answer to my doubts and fears because there, on the edge of that majestic stone I will be able to decipher the ancient hieroglyphs of my existence.

The coffee is hot and I'm waiting for my answers.

There's something different about me. I remember the title of Milan Kundera's book *The Unbearable Lightness of Being*.

The dilemma is still there. What should I choose? Weight or lightness? Parmenides, six centuries before our time, debated the puzzle of contradictions and their opposites: positive–negative, heat–cold, being–not being. At first it might seem childish or banal, but what is negative, the weight on our shoulders? What is positive and bright? Lightness? There's only one thing I'm sure of today and that's that I'm with my ambiguities and contradictions. It's what I feel. I'm free. I don't know how to explain it but my dream was my long walk in the desert with all my ghosts and my judges and with the people I've loved, listening to me, knowing me, and accepting me. They were with me, they spent those hours with me in my dream, they helped me and dried my tears and joined me in my laughter, in my stories, and took my hand to help me climb that pyramid. They assured me there would be no danger, that they were there, their hands and their strength so that I might face up to my past.

They are my present and my continuation. There is an open continuation free from threatening clouds. I believe it. I know it.

"Gabriela, where are you?"

Howard comes into the kitchen and gives me a hug. I can feel the warmth of his body pressed against mine. His pajamas retain the smell of the bed and my own smell. He's barefoot. He has the same toes as my eldest grandson.

I look into his eyes. He smiles at me with the complicity of almost a lifetime.

"You were talking a lot in your sleep. You were crying and laughing like a baby. Aren't you tired after so much agitation? I'm used to hearing you talk but last night it was like a waterfall and in different languages. How many countries did you travel through?"

I hug him. He has very blue eyes with small flecks of gray. He's not bad at all, this man of mine.

"Would you like some tea?"

He sits down, facing the window. The table is very small. There's hardly room for us to sit across from each other.

"I was traveling. Didn't I tell you? Our girls were with me. They're very well. They're good travelers, with the odd exception but overall it was good."

They have a good critical sense, patience…

Howard is shy when it comes to expressing his feelings.

"Do you think this rain is going to last all day?"

The smells of toast, tea, and marmalade create an intimate atmosphere, very much our own. Under the table I rub Howard's feet with mine and he smiles at me mischievously. I can see lines around his eyes and his hair is getting grayer. It shines in the light of the rain. His beard is also going gray and he's beginning to get a double chin. He's good-looking, he has a slight paunch, but what's most important is that he still likes me. He's my husband and I'm his wife. Forty-eight years we've been together. It gives me quite a giddy feeling that figure, forty-eight—it's a lifetime. The force of that thought provides me with energy and a strong desire to keep going. I'm a survivor who wants to continue surviving. The dream opened a door and let in a torrent of energy that has taken hold of me.

I can hear Howard taking a shower. Water everywhere. I wash the plates and let the water trickle through my fingers. I try to catch some drops but they softly slide away, falling to join the other drops waiting to run together to the dry hills of the desert looking for water. I also want to go back to the desert in the south of Israel where silence welcomes me and leads me to the very center of the pyramid that I think I've managed to build.

I'm back now. I had to go to the country of my birth, to be a child, a sister, and much more. Someone once said that we live two lives: the one we actually live and the one we talk about. But which is which? On the way I gathered colors, scents, and images. With them I contrived stories and added experiences. I learned how to read people's eyes and the gestures of strangers and friends. Emotional lexicons and surprises. I keep hidden the secrets that aren't mine but were confided to me. I wept with the fear of not finding my way or the love we all long for. I accepted my mistakes and now I'm back with all that baggage but I feel strong because now I accept simply being.

"When will you be back?" Howard asks while I begin to make the bed. He's looking at me hoping it's going to be one of my unexpected outings that in some way will nurture our relationship.

"Is there anything in particular you want to tell me?"

I like the sheets to be so tight they look almost starched. I shake them out to renew the freshness lost with the night's creases.

I open the window and let in air mixed with drops of rain. I feel free, strong, and wanting to do something out of the ordinary.

I laugh at myself. I have wrinkles and my hair is white. That's why I dye it. My back is still straight. I can run fearlessly toward new frontiers. I keep deep inside me the key to my secret garden.

I don't know how much time I have left but I don't want to measure it too much. It's mine.

"Howard, I want to go to the Negev, take my shoes off, sleep in a tent, prepare tea or coffee while watching the sun rise when in that briefest springtime there's a sea of anemones, the brilliant *calanit*. That, that's what I want."

Made in the USA
Charleston, SC
04 October 2016